MYSTIC

by K. D. Rausin

ISBN: 1480002461
ISBN 13: 9781480002463

Library of Congress Control Number: 2012918302
CreateSpace Independent Publishing Platform
North Charleston, South Carolina

ACKNOWLEDGMENTS

Dreams do come true. Thank you to the following people for believing in MYSTIC.

Patti Gauch: My deepest gratitude for introducing me to the wonderful world of children's fantasy.

Rob Gerth: You always had words of encouragement. Thank you.

Elena Shidel: Sometimes all it takes is a friend telling you not to give up. You have been that friend and so much more.

Emma Dryden: Teacher, guide, editor extraordinaire, thank you for believing in this story and in me.

Eric Rausin: I am blessed, truly blessed with your friendship, support, and love. It's you and me—always.

Kai Rausin: Creative, comedic, and compassionate, my beautiful boy.

Arielle Rausin: My hero. This story is for you. My beautiful girl.

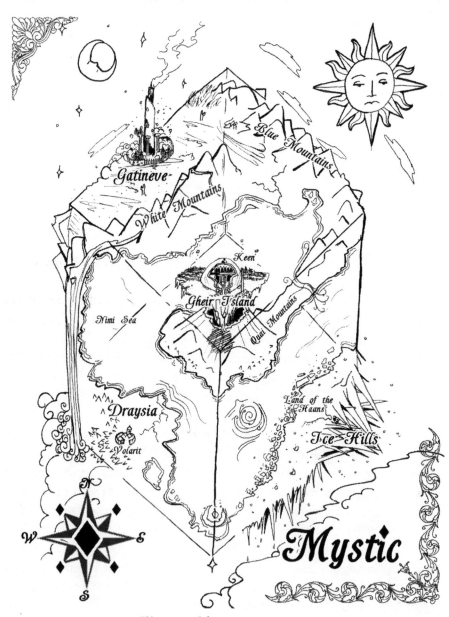

Gatineve

Blue Mountains

White Mountains

Keen

Gheir Island

Nimi Sea

Quai Mountains

Draysia

Volarit

Land of the Haans

Ice Hills

Mystic

Illustrated by Mina Sanwald

CHAPTER I

Amelia wheeled through the classroom door, saw the clipboard on the podium, and knew she was in trouble. A sub.

It was exactly 7:00 AM. Plenty of time to transfer out of her wheelchair to her desk without anyone watching. She hated kids staring at her, feeling sorry for her. She didn't need their pity.

Amelia angled her wheelchair to her seat and scooted to the right. Her body tipped and she flung her arms out to balance herself. "Whew!" she muttered. She didn't end up on the floor—this time. She grabbed her drawstring bag from the handles and shoved the chair so it rolled towards the back corner of the room, under Ms. Russell's *Bloom Where You are Planted* poster.

Some sixth graders bounced through the door, poking and punching one another on their way to their seats. Amelia might as well be a ghost. She knew them, though. Joel, tall and cute; Kevin, who always tapped his pencil on his desk; bossy Amber; and Jay, who picked his nose. They all talked over and around her. She transferred to her seat every day and pushed the wheelchair as far away as possible in hopes of looking normal, but still... What was so hard about saying "Hello," or "Can I copy last night's homework?" She would gladly have handed over all her answers for just one "Hi."

An older man in a pinstriped suit entered the room and wrote MR. NORTON across the board. Amelia sighed and looked around.

Greg was late again. He'd probably heard there was a sub and figured he had plenty of time to stop to talk with Coach T. about summer football conditioning. Football—her favorite sport. She and Greg used to play every day after school. No one had ever wanted them on the same team because they were like Jerry Rice and Joe Montana. She used to outrun any boy covering her, and Greg, knowing just where she'd be, would fire the ball right into her arms. It was as if they could read each other's mind. Maybe it had something to do with the fact that they were born on exactly the same day, January 5th or maybe it was because neither of them lived with their parents. Whatever it was, Greg had been her best friend.

"Young lady, get to your feet and show honor to your country!" Mr. Norton's nasal voice carried over the room like a trumpet in a flute recital. Everyone but Amelia was standing with their right hand flat over their heart.

"Um…she can't." Someone coughed the words. *Just tell him.* The old Amelia would have spoken up, but since the accident eighteen months and five days ago, it was as if she were broken, her voice as paralyzed as her legs. Why couldn't this guy see what was going on?

Stop staring at me, I can't help it. Amelia wanted to scream. Or run away. But she couldn't do either. She watched as the tips of her thumbs turned from pink to white as she pressed them into the pages of *The Hobbit. Focus. Focus on the words, read, escape; you're not really here in this classroom. You're far away in a land where wheelchairs don't exist. One swish of a magic wand and everyone is healed. Don't cry. Don't cry.*

The pledge ended. She felt like she was on stage, with the spotlight burning her face, and she'd forgotten her lines. Humiliating silence. Then, a laugh broke through the room. Not a normal laugh, a forced belly laugh. She looked up.

Greg stood in the doorway, his backpack flung over his shoulder, pointing to the wheelchair. Mr. Norton's face was scrunched so tight his eyebrows touched his nose. "Oh—yes, well. Yes, I see…." He picked up the clipboard, focusing all his attention on the instructions left for him by Ms. Russell. Kids giggled.

"Okay, everyone take your seats. Let's begin."

Amelia set *The Hobbit* down and covered her burning cheeks with her hands. Greg high fived Joel before he sat down next to her.

2

"Thanks," she whispered.

"He's a jerk."

Amelia glanced at the clock. A display of numbers appeared in her mind the way it always did. Two thousand, four hundred seconds until she could leave—only to sit through the next class.

Mr. Norton was still reading through Ms. Russell's notes. Greg held up his English book, imitating Mr. Norton. "Take out your books and turn to page 253. Read the chapter." Greg mumbled and bobbed his head.

Everyone except Amelia laughed. Mr. Norton peered over the clipboard. Greg was a pro. His book was already back on his desk, and his dimple made him look innocent. Mr. Norton went back to reading.

Greg was like the great Dwarf leader in *The Hobbit*, Thorin Oakenshield—important, full of life, a presence wherever he went. And he was her neighbor. She was at 335 Poplar Lane and he was at 228, just a spread-arm away from each other. Greg lived with his Grandma Kent. Once Amelia had asked Greg what happened to his parents. He'd brushed his long bangs out of his eyes and said, "I don't talk about it."

Amelia had fallen in love with Grandma K. at first sight. Something about Grandma K.'s eyes made her feel as though the woman was her Grandma too. Maybe it was love. Amelia wasn't sure. The first time she'd ever seen Greg and Grandma K. was two summers ago, exactly four weeks and one day after Amelia had been sent to the children's group home in Elizabethtown when her foster mom "needed a break." Amelia had looked out her window one morning and had seen a giant Mayflower moving truck parked outside the house down the street where Old Man Rudy had died in his sleep.

Watching the blond boy carry box after box after box into the brown split-level house, Amelia had wondered how two people could have enough stuff to fill a truck that size. She had only two drawers full of clothes, a stuffed dog, and a framed picture of what she imagined her real mother to look like. Really it was just a photo cut from *Home & Garden* magazine.

The next morning, the doorbell had rung. Amelia opened the door and there stood Grandma K., with silver curls popping out of a Philadelphia Phillies baseball cap, black rimmed glasses, and chubby hands holding a vanilla frosted cake with green lettering that said, WELCOME. The boy stood beside her, frowning. He had his hands on his hips.

"Well, hello, darlin'! We knew we were coming, so we baked *you* a cake. Aren't you a beauty? I can tell, you're not foolin' me, there's a secret behind those hazel eyes. Nice to meetcha! I'm Grandma K., darlin'. Meet my grandson, Gregory."

Greg had rolled his eyes to the top of the poplar trees, and Grandma K. had hip-bumped him so big it knocked him sideways. Amelia had just stared and tried not to laugh. She'd never been called beautiful before. And she didn't really have a secret. Well, she'd never told anyone that she *could* memorize books and solve equations faster than a calculator. How could Grandma K. have known about that? Impossible.

Greg had rubbed his hands down his jeans and looked straight at Amelia. That's when she noticed his electric blue eyes. And the difference in their heights. She was a whole foot taller than Greg.

"Who's there, Amelia?" Ms. Linda, the housemother, came downstairs with little Joey trailing behind her.

"Our new neighbors. They brought us a cake."

"Well, invite them in, sweetie. We never refuse cake around here." Ms. Linda motioned for Grandma K. to come in, and the two chatted their way to the kitchen as if they'd known each other their whole lives.

Amelia closed the door then scooped up Joey. Greg tapped his fingers on his thighs.

"Do you have a brother?" he asked.

"I don't think so. This is Joey." Amelia kissed the toddler's cheek. Joey wrapped his arms around her neck.

"Too bad. I like to play football." Greg poked Joey's stomach. "Do *you* like football?" Joey giggled and buried his head in Amelia's shoulder.

"He's shy. And who says you have to be a *boy* to like football? I play all the time with the boys." Amelia had no choice. She was the only girl in the house besides Ms. Linda, so on days when she didn't have to help take care of Joey, she'd join her four housemates, all boys, for a game of two-hand touch. It was the only time they treated her like she belonged. She didn't blame them. They'd already been a family when she'd arrived.

"*The boys?*" Greg had a hint of a smile. Amelia noticed the cute little dimple on his right cheek.

Amelia rubbed Joey's back. She hated the words she was about to say. They tasted bitter, like unsweetened cocoa. "This is a group foster home.

4

I live with a house full of boys…" Amelia hesitated. "But if you ask them who the best football player is, they'll all say it's me."

"Meelya!" Joey threw his arms up into the air. Amelia tickled him.

Greg laughed. "Well, where are they?"

"Umm—probably out back… hopefully lost in the woods." Amelia set Joey down. "Ms. Linda has cake, honey. Why don't you go on?" Joey ran to the kitchen.

Greg yanked on her sleeve. "C'mon, let's find them and get a game going. You're on my team." That was boy talk for "you're cool," and from that day on, they'd been inseparable.

"Hey, Crip, hello? Are you there?"

Crip—that was Greg's new name for her. He used to call her Daddy-long-legs, after the spiders with tiny bodies and string-thin legs that they'd find in their houses. But now it was Crip. She'd been shocked the first time he'd said it. But she knew why he did it. Right after rehab, her first day back to school in fifth grade, she and Greg were in the hallway between classes when they overheard a parent volunteer. "Such a shame that Amelia girl ended up crippled. First an orphan and now this. So awful. Poor, poor girl, what a horrible life. No one's ever going to want her now." Amelia had lifted her legs with her hands, to adjust her feet on the wheelchair's footrest, and hoped Greg would think what they'd heard didn't faze her. But it had. It deflated her like a pin through a balloon. No one would want her. Ever.

Greg had stopped pushing the wheelchair, bent over her, and said, "Don't listen to her. Who wants parents anyway? They make you eat vegetables and get good grades. We're lucky we don't have to put up with them." He'd squeezed her shoulders and tipped the wheelchair back. She'd grabbed her rims and turned her head. She couldn't look at him, or she'd start crying. She replayed the words over and over: *No one's going to want me.* Not that she'd ever thought she'd have a real family anyway—even before the wheelchair. Greg didn't need to see her cry. He'd seen enough of that visiting her in rehab.

"Thanks. Now put me back up, please." Tipping backwards in the chair was still one of the scariest feelings in the world.

"Crippled, crippled, crippled. It's kind of a funny word if you say it quick enough." Greg had pushed her faster down the hall. "Yep, I think I'll call you *Crip* for short."

Amelia knew what he was doing. Taking the sting out of a word that hurt worse than being stung by a hive of angry wasps. It was his way of toughening her up. He knew about being tough, too. Every time a kid talked about their father, Greg cracked his knuckles. Maybe it was harder for a boy not to have a dad than it was for a girl. Maybe.

Greg poked her, bringing her back to the present. "I have to talk to you later," Greg whispered.

"Okay." Amelia glanced at Mr. Norton. Good. He was still oblivious.

Greg was probably going to ask her to write his essay or help him with his math. He knew she was smart, but he had no idea of what she was really capable of when it came to memorization and numbers. And she liked it that way.

The classroom clock clicked to 8:00 AM. Mr. Norton sat at Ms. Russell's desk reading a thick paperback. The rest of the class sat quietly reading, or at least pretending to read, the next chapter in their English book. Amelia had already finished it and could recite every boring word from memory. She closed her English book and grabbed her bag. Life would be so much easier if she could just stand and walk out of the room like everyone else.

CHAPTER 2

Greg knew the drill. As soon as he stood, all eyes were on him as if he were President. She was surprised he didn't take a bow. He would probably grow up to be an actor or comedian. He strolled to the corner to get Amelia's wheelchair. "Beep, beep, beep, coming through." Greg bumped into desks, knocking kids' books onto the floor as he maneuvered the wheelchair to Amelia's side. Jay stared at her as if she were an alien. She pretended not to notice. If only she had an invisibility ring.

"Ahhemmm." Mr. Norton stood up.

"It's okay, Mr. Norton, everything's under control. I'm just getting Amelia to her next class safely."

"*Safely* is quite a relative term, young man."

"Good one, Mr. N...good one. Your chariot, my lady."

Amelia handed Greg her bag, lifted her feet onto the footrest, and slid over onto the cushion. Greg made racecar noises, revving up his engines. Amelia's cheeks burned.

Flinging his backpack on his shoulder, Greg took off, running zigzags down the hall. He pushed her at full speed, aimed directly for a locker, and suddenly turned. The wheels squealed on the polished floor. She gripped the books on her lap and hoped a teacher didn't catch them. Greg only did this on the days he felt she needed cheering up. Sometimes it worked. Today it didn't.

"Stop, you're going to get us in trouble!"

Greg swooshed the back of her hair with his hand. His finger got stuck in one of her jet-black curls. "Ouch! Greg, stop."

"What's the matter, Crip? Why are you so grumpy?"

"I'm *not* grumpy. I'm just...I'm just...oh, whatever."

"Why didn't you stick up for yourself? Or tell Mr. Norton you couldn't stand? You should have made *him* feel like the jerk."

"Pfft—yeah, right."

Greg stopped the chair. Amelia tried to take over, but her hand slipped off the wheel rims. Greg was holding the handles and she couldn't move. He was trying to make her laugh, but he just didn't get it.

"Come on, Greg, knock it off. I have to get to class." She tapped her watch.

The bell rang, and students poured from the doorways into the hall. She was surrounded by bellies and feet. And she was stuck.

Amelia turned to glare at Greg.

He winked at her. "*There* you are. That's the determined Amelia I knew."

She rolled her eyes.

"That's the Amelia who would have stood up for herself to old Mr. Snorin' Norton."

"Stood up? Really?"

"C'mon, you know what I meant..." He tipped her back into a wheelie again.

"You're a brat, Gregory Timothy Chandler!"

And then he did it. He made her laugh. How did he have this power over her? Upside down she stared into his blue eyes and felt a twitch in her stomach. No one could make her feel so completely frustrated one minute and so happy the next. Ms. Linda had once told her that was the "boy" way.

Amelia leaned forward, and Greg lowered the chair so all the wheels were securely on the floor. She spun around to punch him in the arm, and when she turned back, Jenna was heading right towards them. Goblin girl, that's what she was—an annoying goblin. Just when there was a moment of hope that her day would get better, enter Jenna.

Amelia watched the way Jenna swayed and tucked her hair behind her ear as she strutted toward them. Jenna Reese. Aka new-boyfriend-every-two-weeks Jenna. It was obvious Greg was her next target. And here she was coming up to them with her coy turned-up smile that said, "I know I'm so cute."

"Hi, Jenna." Greg put his hands on Amelia's shoulders. What was he doing? She didn't need to be here for this.

"Hi, Greg...hey, did you get the invite to my party next Saturday?" Jenna snapped her gum.

"Party?" She felt Greg's finger tapping her shoulder blade. Were they just going to talk over her as if she weren't there? Oh, please! "Yeah...ah...I think I can come."

"Oh, that would, like, be really great. Oh, I love your hair cut!"

"Ahh—I didn't get my hair cut...it probably just grew longer...in the back."

Amelia felt like puking all over Jenna's Nikes. *Flirt, I'm sitting right here, can't you see me...hello?* Listen to that pathetic fake laugh.

Amelia didn't allow herself to think Greg was cute. Sure, he had blond hair that curled like a wave along his neck. And blue eyes that were actually prettier than the sky. But he was *Greg*—the boy who used to sing, "Take a whiff! Take a whiff!" every time he farted. The boy who made racecar noises and talked to teachers as if they were his best friends. Her friend since they were nine.

"My bad."

Oh, now Jenna had done it. She had used that phrase, that horrifically annoying phrase. Amelia couldn't take anymore. "Ready, Greg? I've got to get to class."

"Oh, hi, Amelia... I'm so sorry I didn't even say hello." Giggle. "My bad again."

Oh, like, hi, Jenna...I know this wheelchair makes me look like I'm not really a person with thoughts and feelings but, guess what? I'm real. They're just wheels and I'm just, like, sitting down.

"See ya, Jenna." Greg pushed Amelia down the hall.

"You didn't give me a chance to say good-bye to your sweetheart," Amelia said.

"She's annoying." Greg flicked her ear.

Really?, he didn't like Jenna? Well, good. He shouldn't go around liking goblins anyway.

"I've got a question for you." Greg pushed her to his locker. The two-minute bell was going to ring any second. She'd be late to class again. At least the wheelchair was good for one thing— teachers never questioned a *helpless cripple* about being late.

Greg opened his locker and looked down at her. She used to be the one who looked down at him. Now he towered over her at five foot eight. She was probably five foot six, standing—maybe. "I want you to come on a camping trip with me and Grandma K." He rummaged around in the locker and grabbed his history book.

"What?"

"I want you to come camping with me in a few weeks, after school's out." He handed the book to her.

"You're insane!"

"Come on, it'll be a blast. Remember last time? We'll be leaving in three weeks for the cabin."

Was he nuts? Did he hear himself? How could she possibly get around the woods in a wheelchair? She'd be stuck in the cabin all week long!

"I can't go." She turned and started wheeling away.

His locker slammed shut. "Why are you so afraid, Mel? I don't even know you anymore. You're so... different."

She swung herself back around. "Greg, I can't stand! I can't walk anymore! I *am* different. Don't you get it? No more football...no more Jerry Rice and Joe Montana...I'm not that Amelia anymore. I'm a cripple—a helpless cripple!"

"You used to be fun! Remember the time we found that mudslide? You were the first to slide down and convince me to try it. We laughed so hard our stomachs hurt, and I had to take three showers to get all the mud off. You weren't afraid to get dirty. You weren't afraid of anything! Now all you do is sit around and read your dumb books about trolls and castles! Most days you don't even smile, Mel."

"I wasn't in a wheelchair last time we went camping. Yeah, Greg, it sucks to be in a wheelchair. It sucks when all your life you've been able to do things like walk, run, and jump and then suddenly have it all taken away and you don't even know why—or what happened. One day you wake up in the woods and you can't move your legs or remember anything. Have you ever heard of that happening? I haven't—except to unlucky me! And, by the way, I *enjoy* reading Tolkien. It's about all I can do anymore."

"You're just like him, you know that? You're just like Bilbo Baggins. All you want to do is sit at home... Forget it! Forget I even asked you!" He stormed off down the hall.

The bell rang. She hoped he got a detention for being late.

She threw Greg's history book after him. "Here! You forgot this!"

How dare he? How dare he make her feel bad for not being able to walk? Didn't he get it? She would give anything to go camping and find another mudslide. She would trade her life in E-town for any life anywhere else if she could just walk again.

Greg was gone. The hall was empty. Amelia had to get to the bathroom and calm down before going to class. She pulled out *The Hobbit*. This book had gotten her through those long days in the hospital and rehab. Every day the nurse had come in and rubbed her ankles. "Any changes? Can you feel this?" Amelia hadn't lifted her eyes from her book. "Honey, I have to give you your shot now. Two a day. I know it's hard. After a few months you won't have to get them anymore. Slight pinch... are you listening to me?" *Gandalf's a wizard! If I were a wizard, I'd heal myself and walk right out of this room.* "Okay, honey—it's okay—tomorrow's a new day. Maybe tomorrow we'll see some changes in your legs. Don't give up hope, honey."

Amelia wheeled to the girl's restroom and swung the door back far enough to get herself through. She wheeled to the last stall—the handicapped stall. But someone was in there. She wheeled over to the sinks. The counter hit her knees. She stretched her hands toward the faucet but couldn't reach. *Dammit!* She couldn't see herself in the mirrors either because she was too low. She ran her fingers through her long hair trying to untangle the crazy curls. Sunlight streamed in through the long rectangular window at the far end of the room. A blue jay was perched on a thin branch. If she could fly...

A toilet flushed. Amelia sat up straight and wiped her eyes.

Jenna came out of the stall, tugging down on her sweater that was two sizes too small. Of all people, why did it have to be her?

"So, I, like, saw you talking to Greg for, like, a long time." Jenna started to rummage through her purse as she talked. She pulled out a lipstick. Not once did she look into Amelia's eyes. She leaned her face close to the mirror and puckered her lips.

"Yeah." Didn't she need to get to class?

"Oh, like, that's so funny. You're so lucky having such a cute guy to take care of you. I wish I was, like, in a wheelchair." Giggle, giggle. "Must be nice."

CHAPTER 3

Amelia couldn't sleep. She lay in her bed listening to the wind and rain rattle the window. Flashes of lightning illuminated the room, reminding her of sitting in a classroom waiting for someone to turn out the lights for a movie. Dark...light...dark. And the thunder after the flash was just like a teacher yelling, "Don't turn off all the lights! Only some of them!" Happened every time.

Everyone, including Ms. Linda, was asleep upstairs. Amelia wondered what Greg was doing. Was he still mad at her? Why'd she been so mean to him? She should've just told him her doctor wouldn't allow her to go on that dumb camping trip or something. Greg deserved to have friends he could do things with. Why did he want her to go, anyway?

Amelia glanced at the cell phone on the table. *Ring. Please ring.*

Rumbles leaped up onto the bed, startling Amelia out of her thoughts. "Hey, boy, are you going to keep me company tonight?" She stroked the cat's long, orange-striped coat. He nudged her chin with his head. Cat drool dripped onto her hand.

"You're my buddy, aren't you?" She wiped her hand on the sheet. *Slam!* The shutters banged against the window. *Slam!* Rumbles scrambled out of her lap and under the bed. The storm was getting worse.

Amelia slid herself sideways onto the wheelchair. *Camping?* Greg was crazy.

Amelia wheeled over to the window and leaned forward to rest her forehead on the cool glass. She cupped her hands around her eyes to try and see through the dark. Lightning lit up the sky. Shadows of swaying treetops danced in the restless wind. And further out, in the woods, giant poplars held the secret of what had happened the day of the accident. As she'd done so many times since, she strained to remember.

She and Greg had been exploring in the woods that day. Greg was ahead, yelling for her to follow him because he said he'd found a secret passage. And the next thing she knew, she was in a hospital bed with Ms. Linda holding her hand. Greg told her later that he'd run back and found her lying on the ground unconscious, soaking wet, not moving. And there wasn't a mark on her.

October 27th—the day she'd taken her last steps. Eighteen months, five days, six hours, and thirty-three minutes ago.

"Meelya?"

Amelia unlocked her bedroom door. Joey, in his racecar footie pajamas, climbed into her lap. She squeezed him tightly and kissed the back of his head. He smelled like baby shampoo. He laid his head down on her shoulder and started to suck his thumb.

"Are you afraid?" He nodded, his little red curls bouncing. "It's okay, Joey. It's only a thunderstorm." She ran her hand up and down his back. Someone used to do that to her when she was little. A woman. It must have been one of her foster moms. Joey twisted around in her lap and tried to push her wheels. "Shh, shh, little guy." Amelia rocked him from side to side and sang the words she remembered so well from, *The Hobbit:*

> *"Back to gardens on the hills*
> *Where the berry swells and fills*
> *Under sunlight, under day!*
> *South away! South away!*
> *Down the swift dark stream you go*
> *Back to lands you once did know!"*

When the toddler's eyes closed, she kept Joey tucked close to her, steadying him with her left hand, and wheeled out her bedroom using just her right hand. Amelia could feel his heart beating steady, strong. He trusted her completely.

All the boys' rooms were upstairs, so she laid him down on the couch in the living room. He was the sweetest pretend little brother in the world. She loved the little freckles dotting his nose. She loved how he called her Meelya. She kissed his forehead. "Good-night, little guy."

Amelia covered him with the quilt that Ms. Linda had crocheted for her when she was in the hospital. Turquoise and black seemed like unusual colors to choose for a quilt. Ms. Linda had tried to talk Amelia into pink or yellow—happy colors, she'd called them. But Amelia was adamant. "Turquoise and black, please."

The grandfather clock chimed once—A familiar sound on sleepless nights.

Joey rolled over on his side with his thumb still in his mouth. Amelia wheeled back to her room and pushed her computers silver "on" button. Might as well keep busy until she felt tired. Nothing happened. "Oh, come on! Don't be broken!"

Amelia waited. She pushed the button again. Nothing. The shutters slammed, followed by a distant whooshing sound.

"Ahhh…meeel…yaaa!"

Someone was behind her. Chills raced up her arms and pricked her neck. She glanced at the clock over her bed, focusing on the minute hand gliding over the Roman numerals. It couldn't be Joey. He was fast asleep. The voice was too high to be Ms. Linda's. No one else was in the room. Amelia exhaled, realizing that she'd been holding her breath. Maybe it was the wind or a cricket or her imagination. Slowly Amelia tapped the keys on her keyboard trying to get the computer to work.

"Help...meee!"

What was going on? The voice sounded like a little girl.

"Find… Ju…piterrr!"

Something was whispering to her through the blank monitor. Leaning as far away from the monitor as she could, her mind was a fuse box of wires short-circuiting. Afraid to turn around, afraid to leave the room, she sat gripping her wheels cold metal rims, knowing she should move but totally unable to do so. She squeezed her eyes shut and waited. Maybe she was dreaming.

She opened her eyes. It *had* to be the storm. The storm was making her hear things that weren't really there. Then she remembered she wasn't alone, after all. Rumbles! Lightning flashed. Rumbles stood in the center of the bed, back arched, fur raised, and bristly tail standing straight up like a torch in the dark.

"It's okay, Rumbles. It's just thunder or the computer. It's—there's something wrong with it." She was getting herself all worked up over nothing. Amelia tried to force a laugh like Greg would've, but air jammed in her throat and the noise came out a pathetic squeal.

Rumbles hissed.

"Come here, boy." Amelia patted her lap. The cat didn't move.

A breeze drifted across the back of her neck. Before she could react, she heard it again.

"Help...meee!" Amelia swung back around to the computer. "Stop it!" she yelled. "Stop it now! Go away!"

Suddenly the screen began flashing. Bright rays of neon green and yellow shot across the room, twirling like a tornado of light and filling up all four corners.

Amelia lowered her head and covered her eyes. *Stop! Please stop!* In the distance she could hear a little girl humming. The tune was familiar. Amelia knew she'd heard it before, but she couldn't remember where. She clutched her stomach. Her body wanted to run away, but she was stuck in her seat unable to move, unable to scream. Amelia covered her face. Then...

Calm. Everything stopped. Amelia felt her hot breath on her hands. This wasn't a dream. Amelia lifted her head and slowly opened her eyes, afraid of what might be standing in front of her. Rumbles jumped on her lap, claws bared, and she let out a squeal. He ran his face along her chin. Movement on the monitor caught her eye. Amelia slid her hand along Rumbles' back and pressed down on his fur to get a view of the screen. It was some sort of picture or film: a giant banyan tree with a braided trunk stood on top of a hill. In the exact center of the tree trunk was a circular crevice, and inside the crevice was a flickering flame of blue, red, and orange.

"Amelia, it's Laural... please help me." This time the voice was a crisp whisper, so clear it tickled her ear. So clear Amelia felt her lips go numb as she squeezed her mouth shut and forced back tears.

Rumbles nudged her chin again. Amelia wrapped her arms around him and buried her head into his side. *Make it stop! Please make it stop!* Rumbles squirmed and tried to break free. Finally Amelia let him go.

When Amelia raised her head again, the image was gone. Now there was only the familiar peaceful starfish sitting on the bottom of the ocean—her screensaver. But she was feeling anything but peaceful. What was happening to her?

Suddenly Amelia felt as though someone was watching her. She looked towards the window. Something was out there. "Ms. Linda!" Amelia yelled as loudly as she could, but still only wisps of air and sound mixed together to form a pathetic whisper. Amelia pushed with her shaky arms, trying to wheel out the door. Lightning flashed again, and this time she saw...

Two yellow eyes with ghostly white ovals were staring at her.

"Ms. Linda!" She had to get out. She pressed harder on her rims. "Go away!" Somewhere deep inside her, anger rose, and she shouted again, "GO AWAY!"

A branch scraped against the glass.

She was yelling at a branch. "Ridiculous. Don't be such a geek." She wiped her eyes. It was time for her to get some sleep. But not in her bedroom. And not alone.

Amelia wheeled to the bed, grabbed her pillow, and set it on her lap. The cell phone started to vibrate. *No, please, not now...* she watched as it jiggled all the way to the edge before she snatched it. She recognized the number. Greg. *Thank goodness.* Amelia held her breath and pushed the green button to answer.

"Hello?"

"Mel, is that you? I know it's late. Look, I'm sorry... I'm sorry for everything. I keep thinking about you, and I can't sleep. Listen, I get it... you don't want to go camping. It's okay. We can do other things this summer."

Amelia felt a tear slide down her cheek. It made a tiny wet circle on her pillowcase. She swiped it away. She wanted to tell him what just happened, but instead she said, "I'm sorry, too." He'd never believe her if she told him what happened. No one would. Then before she could stop herself..."Listen, I've decided to go. I'm coming camping with you." Sleeping anywhere but her bedroom felt like a great idea right now. Ms. Linda loved Grandma K. She'd let her go.

"Really?" Greg's voice went up two octaves. "That's awesome! I'm so excited. We're going to have a blast. Just wait—you'll see. Hey, what made you change your mind? No, it doesn't matter. This is cool. I can't wait to tell Grandma K."

He wasn't mad at her anymore. He was still her friend. That's what mattered most. She couldn't tell him about the voice and the flashing lights, though. How many secrets was she going to have to keep from her best friend? She'd just have to pretend to be normal. Normal? Yeah, right. But it would be the only way she'd keep Greg's friendship, and he was all she had.

"Amelia, are you there? Hello? Earth to Mel…"

"Sorry, I'm tired. It's really late, y'know?"

"Yeah, sorry. Okay—so, goodnight, Mel. I'll talk to you tomorrow. Call me. Bye."

"Bye." Amelia set the phone on the desk. Things were going to get much better. Greg was her friend again. They'd go away as soon as school let out for summer vacation and she wouldn't let herself think about the voice…or those eyes. Thunder groaned, rattling the roof. She got back into bed. *There's no such thing as monsters.*

CHAPTER 4

Three weeks zipped by. Students tossed their notebooks into the air and bolted out the door. Amelia found herself in the backseat of Grandma K.'s Ford Falcon station wagon, counting the number of road signs they'd passed since leaving Elizabethtown: 532. She was sweating in between a dirty red cooler and several knitted blankets shoved up against her thigh and the door. Perry Como's "Magic Moments" crackled through the radio. Grandma K. loved her station wagon and her oldies stations.

The crooning reminded Amelia of the worst four weeks of her life—rehab. She'd waken to the sounds of ancient crooning music and smile because it meant Grandma K. and Greg were at her side. Greg would ask, "Hey, is anything new?" She'd shake her head and watch Greg's shoulders drop forward just slightly. Then he'd hold up a new board game and movie. "For today's activities we have *Ticket to Ride*, followed by physical therapy, followed by Jackie Chan, followed by horrible mystery food prepared by your favorite rehabilitation hospital. Sound like a plan?"

"Awesome." Favorite rehab hospital? Stressed nurses who jabbed shots into her thighs morning and evening, dirty shower chairs that gave her ringworm, screaming kids waking up from comas, babies abandoned by parents too busy to visit, and prisoners housed on the floor above. All of this and she got to learn about digital stimulation and catheters, too. Yes, rehab was just like Disney World. At least she had Greg, whose constant teasing distracted her. Amelia and Greg. Jerry Rice and Joe Montana.

Amelia glanced over at Greg sitting behind Grandma K., his head against the window, mouth wide open. He was out cold, even though Grandma K. was bellowing to the music, both hands firmly on the steering wheel, "Time can't erase the memory of these magic moments..." They were almost to Clarion. The sky was slate gray. Dark clouds loomed far in the distance.

Amelia missed little Joey. He'd cried and wouldn't let go of her when she tried to say good-bye. "Come back! Come back, Meelya!" She knew why Joey screamed. People left him, just like they'd left her. He didn't think he'd ever see Amelia again, and there's nothing like the pain of having someone you love disappear.

Amelia had tried to console the little boy, "I'm coming back Joey! Soon. I'll be back. I promise." He probably hadn't heard her, though. Amelia searched her bag for *The Hobbit* and then remembered. It was sitting on her nightstand, right where she'd left it—on purpose.

Greg gasped in his sleep, opened his eyes, and sat up. She chuckled. He looked funny with his wide eyes staring straight ahead and a small line of drool snaking to his chin.

"Bad dream?"

"Did you *hear* that?" Greg wiped his mouth and then ran his hand down his thigh.

"Perry Como in concert with Grandma K.? Yeah, I've *been* hearing it."

"No, no..." Greg brushed his bangs out of his eyes. "It was a voice... calling for help...and...oh, never mind."

"Go on." Amelia leaned towards him. "What?"

Greg must've been dreaming, but Amelia had to ask—she wasn't so sure she wanted to hear his answer, though. "What did the voice sound like?"

"Never mind—just forget it, OK?" Greg wouldn't look at her. He stared out the window. He brushed his bangs out of his eyes again and sighed. "Do you see the sky up ahead? It doesn't look good." He leaned forward, and spoke loudly to be heard over the crooning. "It looks bad out there, Gram. Maybe we should get off at the next exit?"

Grandma K. kept singing. On key this time. That was a first. "...the time the floor fell out of my car when I put the clutch down...."

"Whatever." He shrugged, sat back, and gazed out the window. His foot started tapping, but not to the music.

Should she tell him? That they'd *both* heard voices? No, he'd think she was making it up to tease him. But, still…they were forever calling each other at identical times as if they'd been reading each other's mind. It wasn't such a big deal.

The car hit a pothole. Amelia flew up into the air and thrust her arms out to balance herself. Greg didn't laugh. Something was wrong. Greg always took every opportunity to laugh at her. She had to ask. "I'm curious. Did you hear a man's voice, because Perry's singing—?"

"It sounded like a kid, like a little girl," Greg interrupted. "She said 'Help me,' and something about Jupiter. Really weird, right?" Greg tried to smile at her. She knew it was fake—no dimple. She swallowed and clenched her teeth. It was exactly the same thing she'd heard!

"I was dreaming," Greg continued, "that you and I were climbing this huge hill and—"

"I was walking?"

Narrow lines crossed Greg's forehead, and his eyebrows dipped toward his nose. She knew that face. It was the one he made every time kids at school used the elevator instead of the stairs. Frustration. She shouldn't have interrupted him.

"Uh, yeah, I guess so. You weren't in your wheelchair, so I guess you were walking. We kept climbing, and this voice came out of nowhere: a little girl calling us and saying 'Jupiter,' and 'Help me, help me'." Greg shrugged. "I don't know…just a silly dream."

Grandma K. glanced over her shoulder. "Ewwweee! Get ready, you two—we're in for some trouble up ahead. Those clouds are darker than molasses on burnt toast." Then she went on singing. "…the Halloween hop when everyone came in funny disguises…"

Greg's dream couldn't be a coincidence. What if it really hadn't been a tree branch that had frightened her? What if those eyes had been real and something was…watching them?

Greg stretched and grunted. "Must be riding so long in this car, listening to this ancient music and Gram's singing… it's getting to me."

Amelia faked a laugh. "Yeah." She was afraid to open her mouth again for fear of what would spew out. Her stomach roiled uncomfortably, like she'd swallowed a spoonful of fish oil and mayonnaise.

21

Only a sliver of light escaped along the edges of the dark clouds, and Grandma K. belted the end of the song as they drove right into the storm. "… magic moments filled with love."

Amelia gripped the door handle, listening to the bullets of rain crashing down on the metal roof. This was all too familiar. The storm, the voice…She turned to look out the rear window, but boxes and the wheelchair blocked her view.

"Hey, Mel, what's there to eat?"

How could Greg be thinking about food right now? Should they tell Grandma K. about the voice, and should she mention the eyes? Would Grandma K. be able to protect them? Going to a cabin in the woods now seemed like the worst idea ever.

Greg persisted. "Earth to Mel… Are you there?" He rummaged through the cooler. "Is this your cheese and pickle sandwich?" He tossed her the sandwich. Then he fished out some chocolate chip cookies and shoved two into his mouth.

"That's disgusting." Amelia tried to sound normal as possible. As if some horrible monster wasn't after them.

"And yummy!" Bits of cookie spewed out of his mouth onto the vinyl seat.

She stared at her sandwich and then back outside. She could still see the mountains. At least it wasn't completely dark. Lightning flashed. Grandma was here, Greg was here. *Relax. Everything's going to be okay.* That's what Grandma K. had said when she'd first come to the hospital to see her. "Everything's going to be okay."

Amelia opened the plastic baggie and took a bite, hoping her stomach would accept the sandwich. Back and forth, back and forth, the windshield wipers moved the raindrops from side to side. *Swish-hit! Swish-hit! Swish-hit!* The rain persisted, and no matter how hard the wipers worked the rain kept coming, making it nearly impossible to see.

Jagged gray rock surrounded them. Two lanes of traffic heading north towards New York were separated by a median from two lanes of traffic heading south to Pennsylvania. Slopes of mountains lined the outer sides of the highway making Amelia feel as though she were a mouse traveling through a giant maze. No exits. She was trapped. Wildflowers—brilliant purple, gold, and red—decorated the grassy median, but they were bending helplessly against the strong gusts of wind.

Grandma K. turned down the music and took off her baseball cap. That was strange. Grandma K. never took off her cap; she always said it was bad luck.

"Grandma K., is everything all right?" Amelia tried to lean forward, but the seatbelt locked and forced her back.

"Can't talk now, darlin'. I've got to concentrate on the road. It's slick out there."

It was Amelia's only chance to say something. Get it all out. Tell them about that night. Maybe they'd believe her and turn the car around. Or she could say she was sick. Then Grandma K. would have to take them back to Elizabethtown. But what would Greg do? He'd be so mad at her; he'd never forgive her if she played sick.

"It's five after five; we only have about two and half more hours until we reach Brocton." Lightning flashed again, followed by a long crack of thunder. "I don't like this. As soon as I see an exit, I'll pull off. We can find a diner and chow on some pie while we wait for Mother Nature to get it all out of her system."

That was Grandma K. A slice of shoo fly pie could make everything all better.

Greg reached across the seat and flicked her on the arm.

"Hey!" She tried to punch him back, but he was too quick. He slid to his corner and pressed his body against the door.

"You know I'll get you back. Just when you think you're safe...*Bam!*"

"Pfft. Good luck with that." Greg pressed his earphones into his ears and stuck his tongue out at her.

"Oh, that's so mature. Brat!"

Amelia rested her head against the window and watched the drops of rain slithering down the glass. Occasionally, the trail of two or three raindrops would join together like tributaries of a river and flow out of sight. She closed her eyes, absorbing the hum of the old station wagon. Maybe her imagination was getting the best of her. Maybe what she needed was some sleep, and then she'd realize everything really *was* okay.

CHAPTER 5

"**S**top the car! Stop the car!"

Amelia's eyes shot open. Greg was screaming, and the car was spinning in circles. Lightning flashed like a strobe light, making it impossible for Amelia to piece together where they were. She stretched to the ceiling to try and hold her body in place, but the spinning was too great, and her head lobbed to the side and hit the window.

"Grandma, make it stop! Brake! Brake!"

Amelia pushed harder against the ceiling and tried to raise her head. It worked. The cooler slammed into her ribs, then fell back towards Greg. "Greg, look out!" It was too late. Her wheelchair crashed down on top of the cooler, and the footrest hit Greg in the face. His head fell forward, and his eyes closed.

"Help! Grandma K., stop the car! Greg's hurt! Stop!"

Grandma K. was frantically turning the steering wheel to the left and to the right.

"Stop!"

Lightning flashed and that's when she saw it on the hood of the car. The yellow eyes—peering in through the windshield, staring right at her!

"Ahhhhhhhhhhhh!" Amelia's scream was sharp. Her stomach clenched, and her mouth stayed open long enough for the cheese sandwich to spew out all over her lap and the seat in front of her.

25

Amelia wiped her mouth and closed her eyes. *Leave me alone!* Her throat burned. *Leave me alone!* Tires squealed. Thunder crashed. She opened her eyes and raised her head. The car was zig zagging down the road. Amelia gripped the door handle. Lightning flashed. She gasped. The creature's gaze was piercing. Sharp-pointed fangs extended from the top of his massive mouth.

Grandma K. mumbled in raspy whispers—words that made no sense: *"Sei debole, sono forte!"*

"What's that? What're you saying?"

Lightning flashed, revealing black and gold striped wings covering the hood and disappearing down the sides of the car. "Faster, Grandma K.! Get it off the car! Don't let it get me!"

But no matter how much Grandma K. spun the wheel, the monster wouldn't let go. It wouldn't move its gaze from Amelia. *Go away! Please go away!* Amelia covered her head and screamed as loudly as she could.

The car jolted, crashing into something. Amelia flew forward for a second, then slammed back into the seat. Glass exploded and shards dropped down onto her body. Amelia listened. Was it still out there? Was it dead?

Rain continued to ping on the roof of the car. Amelia felt her chest rising and falling. *I'm still alive.* Slowly she sat up and uncovered her face. Her hands shook uncontrollably as she tried to swipe at pieces of glass. The cooler was halfway through the windshield, and a thick branch was sticking right into the driver's seat. But…where was Grandma K.?

"Grandma K.?"

Amelia listened for sirens, someone coming to help them. Nothing.

"Greg?"

Nothing. Rain poured down, and flashes of lightning illuminated the bent and broken pieces of metal and glass that were once a car. She had to get to Grandma K. Amelia turned her head towards Greg, and a piercing pain shot up her neck. She bit down on her lip and tasted blood. "Greg!" The wheelchair's footrest dangled beside him. His face was striped with lines of red. He wasn't moving. "Greg!" She tried to say more, but her mouth felt like it was packed with sand.

She coughed and wiped the saliva off the side of her mouth. No signs of Grandma K.

What if the monster had taken Grandma K. and was coming back for them?

"Greg," she croaked. "Wake up."

If she could wake Greg, he could help her find Grandma K. *If.*

"Oh, God, please…" she moaned.

Amelia's eyes were heavy and her body numb. All she really wanted to do was sleep; lay her head against the window and rest. Someone had to have witnessed the accident. Help was surely on the way.

Lightning flashed. It frightened her to see Greg so helpless, so pale. *Help him!* A voice screamed through her incoherent thoughts, telling her to do something, anything. Amelia unhooked her seatbelt. She leaned towards Greg, used the blanket to brush glass off the seat, and then pushed down with all her strength, forcing her legs to follow. Good. She was next to Greg. Amelia managed to grab the wobbly wheelchair, raise it over her head, and duck under. She lifted it even higher, bringing it up onto the seat next to her.

"Greg? Greg, are you okay?" Amelia shook his shoulder. His body slumped sideways, and his head fell against the window. "Greg! Come on! Greg!" Drops of blood trickled down the inside of his window, mirroring the raindrops on the outside.

"Greg, wake up! Wake up! Answer me, Greg!" He was fine—he had to be. This couldn't be happening.

"Please!"

His hand twitched.

He was alive!

"Oh, thank you, thank you! Greg, please move your hand again. You can do it." Greg, open your eyes. Please open your eyes! Amelia waited, tears welling. Greg's hand shot to his forehead.

"Yes, that's it! You're okay! Open your eyes!" Greg groaned. "Greg, we've been in a really bad accident. You have to help me find Grandma K."

He slowly opened one eye and then the other. "Good, that's it… Greg, listen to me, we have to find Grandma K. I don't know where she is." He was sickeningly white with two trails of blood running down either side of his nose to the corners of his mouth. Greg pulled his head upright and moaned. "It's just a little cut. It's not bad." She lied. She didn't want to scare him. "Can you move your legs?"

Greg lifted his left knee and then his right leg. "Good, now use your shirt to wipe your face." He lifted his T-shirt to his forehead and dabbed at the blood, grimacing in pain. "Greg?" He still seemed dazed and zombie-like, but she needed him to go outside and look for Grandma K.

"What happened? Where are we?" Greg winced every time his shirt touched his face.

"We were in an accident. We hit a tree in the median. I think we're in New York. Greg, I don't know where your grandma is."

"Grandma!" Suddenly Greg was lucid and before Amelia could say another word, he opened his door and fell to the ground. Rain flattened his hair to his face and washed off the blood.

"Greg, wait!" Amelia twisted around to grab the metal bars above the footrest. Her arms ached, but she managed to lift the wheelchair over her body and out the door. Rain soaked the black fabric and her wheels sunk down into mud. "Oh, no!" she muttered. It was going to be near impossible to wheel herself in this mess.

Amelia scooted herself across the seat towards the door, her motionless legs dragging behind. She reached out, scooped up her legs and aligned them with the rest of her body. Greg was yelling for her, but she could only see his outline when flashes of lightning lit up the sky. He was crumpled on the ground, kneeling over something. Lightning blinked again. She saw Grandma K.'s white curls. She wasn't moving.

Amelia's wheelchair sat on the ground waiting for her. She gripped the door handle and hesitated. *Please, please let Grandma K. be alive.* Maybe she should stay in the car. Maybe she couldn't handle seeing Grandma K. like that. Maybe that thing was still out there waiting for her. Greg screamed her name. Amelia couldn't move. Why weren't there any cars on the highway? Where was everyone? Greg yelled again. "Amelia! Hurry!"

Amelia's mind screamed, *Help him!* and she felt her body moving despite her panic. She locked the brakes, lowered her body into the chair, wrestled her legs in front of her, and positioned her feet. Cold rain drenched her hair and face. Lightning sizzled through the sky. She tried to move the wheelchair. Her hands slipped on the metal rims and, she rubbed her hands on her sopping jeans. *Push harder, push harder!* She popped a small wheelie and, with trembling arms forced the wheels to move forward.

Greg's pleas got louder. "Grandma, please be okay! Gram, it's Greg. Grandma!"

"Greg, is she all right? I'm coming as fast as I can!"

Mud oozed down her hands and filled her fingernails. Her hands slipped again and hit the brakes, tearing the skin between her thumb and finger. Rain stung the open wounds, but she kept going.

Greg knelt over Grandma K., twenty feet from the car. Amelia swallowed hard, pushed back her tears. Why hadn't she said something when she'd had the chance? Why hadn't she made them turn around and go back home? This accident was all her fault.

Amelia braked when she reached Greg and slid down from her seat, panting, trying to catch her breath. One headlight was shining on Grandma K. She looked peaceful lying there in the rain. Too peaceful. Greg's hand was trembled as he tapped her shoulder. "Grandma, please! It's Greg. Wake up, Grandma, please!"

Amelia felt numb. Greg turned to her. His face was smeared with slashes of mud. The pupils of his eyes covered all hints of blue. She couldn't speak.

"Help her, Amelia, please help her! You're smart—do something! Anything!"

Amelia placed her hand over Grandma K.'s. The woman's skin felt like slippery wax paper. "Grandma K.? Can you hear me?" Grandma didn't move. Amelia lifted Grandma K.'s head gently and wiped her cheeks. "Grandma—we're here. Open your eyes." Nothing. Amelia placed Grandma K.'s head back down, making sure there were no rocks underneath.

"She fainted, right? So, how do we wake her up? What should we do?" Greg stared at his Grandma. "Grandma! C'mon—wake up! WAKE. UP!"

Amelia's leg started to spasm. She didn't care. She knew Grandma K. was gone. She'd felt for a pulse when she'd lifted her head, and felt nothing. She couldn't tell Greg. Saying it out loud would make it real, and maybe none of this was real. Just like the voice and the monster weren't real. Why wasn't anyone coming to help them? Surely some car would have witnessed the accident and called it in by now.

Amelia tried to convince herself that Grandma K. was taking a nap right there in the median, her Phillies cap beside her, comfortable in jeans and a short-sleeved T-shirt that said, *Because I can.* It's something Grandma K. would have done on any given day—lie down in the rain and stare at the sky for no apparent reason. That's what made her so lovable.

Amelia put her hand over Greg's that held Grandma K.'s. The three of them, they were a family. The only family Amelia had. They'd been there for her in the hospital, in rehab, in school, always making her laugh, always telling her that the wheelchair didn't matter. Now, there was nothing she could do to help. Nothing.

They needed a miracle. "I'm sure help is on its way, Greg."

"I'm not waiting!" Greg kissed his grandmother. A drop of blood from his forehead dripped just below Grandma's eye, creating a ruby red tear that slid down her cheek and off her chin. "You stay here with her in case she wakes up."

"What? Where're you going?"

Without a word, Greg stood and took off running.

"Greg, no! Don't go!" That thing could still be out there! "Please, Greg, someone will find us and help us! Greg, it's not safe! Come back!"

But with each flash of lightning, he was further away, running towards the highway. Amelia studied the sky and saw only drifting gray clouds, no wings, no yellow eyes, but she knew it was out there. She couldn't explain it, she just felt it. It was the same feeling she'd had that night. An eeriness, a darkness.

Amelia stared at Grandma K. and felt a boiling anger rise up inside her. Why did she always have to say good-bye? Good-bye to people she thought were her forever parents, good-bye to one home after another, good-bye to walking, running, football, and now good-bye to Grandma K.! Amelia screamed at the top of her lungs. "Help us!"

Because I Can. The words on Grandma K.'s shirt seemed to be speaking to her. Grandma K. would want her to go after Greg.

"Grandma K., he shouldn't be out there alone. You saw the monster. I know you did." Amelia grabbed the chair, lifted her butt up to the footrest, and pushed down until her body bounced onto to the soaked seat. "I'll find Greg, Grandma K... I'll go find Greg and we'll get help for you!" Talking to Grandma K. made it seem as though nothing had changed—Grandma K. was fine. That's what she was going to believe. She pushed herself, hands slipping with each turn. She didn't care. She was going after Greg.

◆

CHAPTER 6

"Greg, stop!" Amelia tried to scrape the mud, rocks, and dirt clinging to her wheels, wincing from the sting of her open wounds. She leaned back into a wheelie again to get through the muck.

A gust of wind blew rain into her eyes. She lowered the front wheels. Her arms were like limp spaghetti. Thoughts of the monster lingered. Was it her imagination, or could she really feel its presence lurking, eyeing its prey?

"Greg!"

Amelia looked up at the sky. She was sure she saw movement—a wave lifting and descending like a giant wing. At any moment, those eyes would appear. Shaking started in her left leg, which spasmed, and continued into her right. Tears followed, uncontrollable tears.

You can make it stop...make it all go away.

A woman's voice came from behind her.

Amelia whirled around. No one.

Amelia heard the call of a bird, long and sharp. And then, the rain just...stopped. She ran her hands over her tires, feeling the pebbled mud wedged into the rubber. She was totally stuck. Trapped.

"I want to go home!" Screaming the words made her feel better.

A bright, jagged light flashed, leaving behind red spirals. Like ribbons or taffy, they twisted and turned, stretching as far as she could see. It wasn't lightning. It was magical. It was beautiful. And as she watched, the swirls joined end to end to form a perfect circle.

Amelia couldn't take her eyes off the glowing circle that was now rising from the bottom, pointing into the center and forming two semi-circles. The semi-circles morphed into a single line that snaked through the sky, turned itself vertical, and twisted towards the ground. The light was heading right for her.

"Greg!" Flashes of neon green and yellow blinded her. Pain pierced her temples, and she covered her eyes. Too bright! These lights were familiar. They were the very same that had filled her room the night she'd heard the voice.

Amelia peeked through her fingers. The red swirl slithered faster and faster towards the ground, as thin as a string and as fast as a snake pursuing its prey. In a few seconds it would be all over.

"Amelia!"

Amelia whipped her head around. "Who's there?" *Move! Move!* "Greg? Where are you?"

The red string was getting closer, lighting patches of grass along the median like a helicopter's spotlight. The wind pushed against her. She leaned from side to side, hoping to pop the wheels out of the mud, but they only sunk down deeper. "Greg! Help me! I'm stuck!"

"Amelia!"

The wind pinned her to her seat. Heat came from the red glow, warming her forehead and cheeks. *Push! Get away!*

"Where are you, Greg?" It was too late. The string was over her, covering her in the hot red light. Her wheels lifted off the ground. Amelia grasped her tires.

"Amelia! No!" Greg appeared, latching his hands around her wrist.

"Greg!"

He tried to pull her towards him, but the wind kept her body glued to her seat, and she was pulling *him*. He managed to hop onto the footrest, but the chair didn't budge. They were two feet off the ground and engulfed in the light. Greg's hair was plastered to his face, and his bangs hung down over the gash in his forehead.

Her stomach clenched. "Jump!" He had to let go, or the light would take him too. It wanted her, not Greg. She'd already caused enough trouble by agreeing to go camping. It was too late for Grandma K. but not for Greg. "You've got to go!" Greg didn't move. "Jump down! Go back to Grandma. Leave me."

"You know Grandma K.'s gone. That's why you couldn't do anything to help her, Mel. I'm staying with you." He leaned toward her. "It's just you and me now."

He knew he was an orphan too. Below them, in a spotlight of scarlet, were four wheel tracks and two footprints etched in the quickly drying mud. She could only watch as they disappeared from sight.

Greg looked like a zombie with his body stiff and arms outstretched as he held onto her. She forced a smile to try to calm him even though her stomach could let loose at any second. Clouds drifted by, outside the glow of the light. Three thousand, four thousand feet—how high were they? She gave Greg's arm three short squeezes hoping for some sort of reaction. Nothing. Maybe he was in shock. Maybe she was in shock. At least she wouldn't feel anything when they hit the ground. It would be over quickly.

Greg opened his mouth.

"What, I can't hear you!" she shrieked.

A sudden gust of wind broke the grip of his right hand, and Greg's body swung out to the side. Amelia clutched the tire in her right hand and grabbed onto him with her left. The chair tipped forward. "Hang on!"

It's happening. This is it!

Amelia felt herself falling from the chair. She clung to Greg's left arm, dangling like a leaf. "Greg, help! Help us! Please, someone—help us!" Her arms couldn't hold on anymore. Then, just as she was about to let go, the wind stopped.

Greg grabbed her. They were face to face, with their bodies free like two skydivers floating above the clouds. Without parachutes.

Amelia's heart pounded so fast she couldn't speak. Instead, she concentrated on Greg's blue eyes and tried to steady her breaths. "I told you camping would be an adventure!" Greg shouted. Amelia nodded. They were still alive.

The heat from the red light burned her cheeks now. They stopped in midair and for a moment—silence. Greg's nails dug into her arm. Both of them looked down at the same time. Nothing except scarlet light.

"Greg?" Amelia met his gaze. His eyes said it all. He knew as well as she did what was coming.

"Noooo!"

They were falling!

CHAPTER 7

Amelia panicked and let go of Greg. Her arms flailed, her body twisted and turned. At first she tried to fight it, to keep herself upright, but it was no use. Air rushed past her, forcing itself into her nose and mouth and stinging her eyes, which she refused to close.

"Amelia!" Greg's cry echoed above her. Head first…roll…feet first…roll…down and down she tumbled. Amelia screamed with everything she had left. And then…

Splash!

The ferocious force of water hit her feet and rose up to her head.

Her mind was still whirling even though her body was upright and sinking. She was alive! Her wheelchair was gone! Cool water soothed her burning cheeks. Down, down. The water was clear as glass. Her black hair flowed out around her face like the curly tentacles of an octopus. Tiny brightly-colored fish, no bigger than her thumb, swam all around her.

Her clothes acted as weights, pulling her deeper. Amelia couldn't hold her breath much longer. She felt the water move above her and looked up. Greg! She raised her arms and pushed out and down, trying to raise her body to the surface. She did it over and over, but the weight of her clothes and her useless legs kept pulling her down. In seconds, Greg was beside her, wildly flailing his arms and legs, but it was no use, he was sinking too. The more he fought against the water, the deeper he sank.

They were like bricks in this ocean or whatever it was. Amelia's lungs were betraying her. She couldn't hold her breath any longer. Pain pierced her chest, and panic flowed like blood through her veins. Air— she needed air!

And then, from the depths of the water, a creature miraculously appeared between Amelia and Greg. Its eyes were huge. Its body ten feet long and six feet wide. Black diamonds adorned a turtle-like shell. The creature—Amelia was sure it was female—smiled serenely and stretched her long, scaly front legs under Amelia and Greg, lifting them up. Amelia's legs slid out in front of her, enabling her to perch on the creature's right leg while Greg balanced on the left.

"Breathe, children," the creature said in an eloquent soft voice. "Just breathe."

Amelia gazed at her. It spoke. The giant turtle creature spoke—underwater, as clear as on land. The giant turtle creature spoke.

"You are safe now. Take a breath."

Amelia sucked in air through her nose, waiting for searing pain to shoot up her face and explode in her head. But instead, fresh, cool, salty air filled her chest. She was breathing underwater!

She breathed deeper. Never had she been so grateful for a single breath. Greg's chest was rising towards his shoulders with every exaggerated breath he took. He glanced at the tortoise. The massive creature bowed her head. Long white eyelashes sparkled like the diamonds on her back.

"Come, children, there's someone I want you to meet."

The tortoise's eyes were calm and soothing, as if they had a story to tell, as if she were a long lost friend. Amelia realized she was feeling just the way she had the day she first met Grandma K., as though they'd already met. Strange. Amelia put her hand over her heart. It was still beating.

The tortoise swam easily towards the surface, keeping Amelia and Greg on top of her legs, rising and falling gently with each stroke.

"Whoa!" Greg's hand shot to his mouth. "We can talk underwater. How cool is that? Going up! No one's ever going to believe this, Mel. We're riding a sea turtle elevator!"

The light had changed from scarlet and shone down on the glass-clear water in rays of gold. The colors of all the creatures that swam around them were magnificent. Blues, golds, red—it was an undersea rainbow.

Massive swirls of water were heading towards them. It looked like a gang of torpedoes. What were they? Whales? Amelia pointed. "Greg!" But he wasn't paying attention to her.

Out popped a half-man/half-dolphin from behind him. Greg took one look and bolted towards Amelia, yelling "Shark!" Amelia laughed so hard she lost her balance and fell sideways. Greg swam right past her, off the tortoise's leg, and immediately began sinking once more.

"Greg! Hey, Greg's in trouble. Please help him!" Amelia waved her arms to get the creature's attention, but the tortoise's head was pointed towards the surface.

The dolphin-man winked at Amelia. "Stay here, I'll get him."

"Ahh...o...ok. Thank you." Her cheeks burned.

Amelia watched as his ponytail swished through the water, and his muscular arms scooped up Greg and carried him back. Why hadn't she gone after Greg? Then she would have had to be rescued, too. Her stomach twirled as the dolphin-man approached and several more suddenly appeared beside him.

"Children, these are the Haans. You're safe with them." The tortoise bowed her head. "Haans, your help and protection are much appreciated." Their hair gleamed like the tattooed purple cross on their dorsal fin. They were beautiful. Muscular, handsome, some had long hair, some short, all as colorful as the creatures that filled the sea around them. What was this place?

The Haan who'd saved Greg spoke. "We have secured the perimeter. You should be safe for a short time longer."

"Thank you," the tortoise replied. "Gheir Island will arrive at any moment." Then, she turned. "Amelia, Gregory, as I said before, there is someone I want you to meet. We must be on our way." She lifted her legs, and Amelia felt her body rise through the water.

Greg was eyeing all the Haans and sticking close to Amelia. "Can you believe this? This is awesome! Way better than Minecraft."

CHAPTER 8

They burst through the surface of the water. Bright light blinded Amelia, and she squinted, waiting for her eyes to adjust. A wave splashed over her, leaving the taste of salt. A cool breeze brushed her cheeks. Dangling her useless legs below her, she sculled her aching arms to keep her body upright. What was she going to do when they reached land? She didn't want Greg to have to carry her. That would be humiliating. Questions rolled around in her brain like marbles. Had anyone found Grandma K.? Where were they? How were they going to get home?

Greg dipped his head back in the water and ran his palm across his bangs, pushing them out of his eyes. Amelia noticed that the gash on his forehead was gone. Not a mark. Maybe it hadn't been as bad as she thought.

The tortoise stuck her long wrinkled neck high into the air and blinked. "It's a beautiful day, is it not? Do you feel today's beauty?"

Amelia looked over at Greg who was raising his eyebrows as if to ask, "Is this reptile crazy?" Amelia shook her head to stop him.

The tortoise continued. "Gregory and Amelia, welcome to Mystic."

Greg raised his hand. Oh, no. What was he doing now? "Ahh… question." Greg cleared his throat. Amelia gritted her teeth. *Not now, Greg. Not now.* The tortoise slowly turned her head. "Yes, Gregory?"

"It's Greg, and I'm confused. Are we dead? Did we die in that car accident like Gram? Is Mystic this ocean? Are we ever getting out? I'm getting really wrinkly. Kind of like you."

Amelia glared at Greg. Sometimes he could be so clueless! It was not cool to insult the one who'd just saved them. He should know that.

The tortoise laughed, a gurgling sound like a babbling brook. Amelia exhaled. Thank goodness. Only Greg could spout off insults and get a laugh in return. The tortoise pointed a long foreleg at the sky. "You are very much alive. Mystic is a world, like your Earth—but different in many ways."

"No kidding!" Greg interjected.

"This is the Nimi Sea," the tortoise continued, "and coming towards us is Gheir Island. There you can dry off out of the water and not worry about wrinkles, Gregory."

Swirls of blue, fuchsia, and neon green moved across the sky. It reminded Amelia of a photo she'd seen of the Northern Lights. Was the tortoise saying an island was up *there*? Couldn't be. She scanned every direction and didn't see any land, only gentle flowing waves. Greg was about to say something, when suddenly all of the Haans leaped into the air, flipped head over tail, and splashed back into the water headfirst.

"Wonderful! Thank you, my friends, for your help." The tortoise bowed her head once more. They shot back into the air and bowed towards her, then disappeared under the sea. Two seconds later, their dorsal fins popped up a hundred yards away. They looked like a fleet of racing sailboats, specks of purple gleaming off their crosses.

"Your guide is waiting for you on Gheir Island. Come, children. I'm sure you have many questions, but let's save them for later, shall we? First we must get you adorned with proper attire suitable to Mystic. It will make your stay here more enjoyable, as your new clothes will adapt to any temperature."

Greg gave Amelia a look. "What'd she just say?"

"I think she said we've got to change our clothes." *Who cares what I'm wearing?*

"Um… really, but no, thanks. I'm good. I'm fine in my jeans." Greg pushed against the water, forcing his body backwards, away from Amelia and the tortoise, who were bobbing up and down. "All I ever wear are jeans and T-shirts. In fact…" Before Greg could finish, the tortoise nodded and blinked her eyes. Amelia felt a rush of water swirling around her, pressing up against her. She couldn't see anything. *Stay calm.* She could hear Greg yelling. "Hey, stop…what are you doing to her? Stop!"

Amelia reached out through the spray. The whirl of water disappeared as quickly as it had begun. Amelia wiped her face.

"Look at you, Amelia, all grown up," the tortoise said. "The resemblance is amazing."

Greg was gaping at her.

"What?" she asked. Then she saw she was clad in a beautiful turquoise garment—a one-piece suit of some kind. A strand of her wet hair was caught on something at the back of her neck and Amelia felt a smooth silk collar with a diamond appliqué in the center. The suit hugged her body, but felt more like a bathrobe than a wetsuit. Sparkling black diamonds, exactly like those on the tortoise's shell, decorated the sleeves. She braced herself for Greg's comment. "Oh, go ahead, just say it. I look ridiculous."

"Magnificent! Doesn't she look simply magnificent?" The tortoise spoke over Greg's stammering.

His eyebrows were raised. He was probably thinking of the perfect comment. "You look like Rainbow Fish with all those sparkling diamonds," or "Too bad you're missing the diver's mask, covering your face would be an improvement." Amelia waited.

Greg touched Amelia's right sleeve and paused at her wrist. "What's that on your arm?"

What, no comment about the costume? Amelia lifted the cuff to reveal an odd silver bracelet hugging her skin. Fine silver wires formed two rows of overlapping circles. In the center of each circle was a shiny bead that conjoined three circles. She counted the colored beads: fourteen.

"Whoa...what is it?" Greg fingered some of the beads. "This one's my favorite." He tapped an orange one.

"Be careful, Gregory." The tortoise swam towards them and nodded at Amelia, who was figuring out that her new outfit was actually keeping her upright and buoyant, just like a life jacket. Her arms could rest, and she didn't have to worry about her legs at all. Nice!

Greg persisted. "What is that thing? Turn it around, Amelia. I want to see the other beads."

Amelia pushed the bracelet around her wrist. All the glowing colors reminded her of bright fireworks, which reminded her of home. The thought stung.

"That, Gregory, is called an Ayer. It is quite powerful."

Amelia pulled her cuff down over the Ayer, wondering if powerful meant dangerous. Maybe it would be best to pretend it wasn't even there. A green light glowed through her sleeve. *Okay, ignore the glowing light shining from your wrist.*

"What does the Ayer do?"

"That's for Amelia to determine, and you will find out in time, Gregory. Now it's your turn."

"Oh, no. Like I said, I'm happy in my j—"

The tortoise blinked her long lashes at Greg. Amelia knew what was coming. This was going to be good. Water spouted up into the air and swirled around Greg. She could hear him calling out, "Oh, c'mon! This isn't funny, Mel! I hear you laughing."

He looked—handsome. His blond hair was completely dry and neatly brushed. His wetsuit was russet with yellow diamonds along the sleeves. It didn't have a high collar like hers; instead, it fit tightly against his chest, making him look a little broader than he actually was. Amelia didn't know what to say. *You look really handsome?* No, that wouldn't work.

"You look...ahhh..." Amelia thought Greg could see right through her. She felt funny. She turned her head. *Think of something to say—hurry!* "Dapper! You look very dapper." *Dapper?* Did she really just say *dapper?* Who says that? Geeks say *dapper* and she felt like a huge geek. The tortoise was gazing at her kindly. Amelia had a feeling the creature knew just what she was thinking.

Greg shook his head and yanked up his sleeve. "Hey! Cool! Look at *my* Ayer." He ran his fingers along the silver wires.

Greg's Ayer was totally different from Amelia's. Instead of beads, his bracelet had carved images of animal faces: a hawk, a wolf, and a bear all with glowing eyes. It reminded Amelia of Native American artwork on totem poles. She knew the wolf represented loyalty. That was Greg, all right. "It is a gift, a very powerful gift from Mystic, Gregory. You will know when to use it."

"How?"

The tortoise ignored him. "Come, children, we must hurry." She moved through the waves like an Olympic swimmer. There wasn't anywhere else to go. They had to follow her.

Barely moving her arms in a breaststroke, Amelia glided through the water like a fish. She liked the breeze across her face and the feeling of freedom, but she couldn't shake her nagging thought that once they got to land, she'd be stuck and completely helpless.

Light was fading. Amelia had no idea how much time had passed since the accident. It felt like hours, maybe days, for all she knew.

Mystic's sky was constantly changing colors; lines of silver and blue replaced the fuchsia and neon green. A dark shadow overhead drifted towards them. Another storm? They kept swimming.

"Amelia! Hurry! Catch up!"

Amelia tried to swim faster, but the waves were growing higher. The object in the sky was getting closer, casting a gigantic shadow across the sea. Chills raced through her. This was no storm. She thought of her cozy bed. How nice it would be to just climb under the covers and pull the blankets up over her head. Now, she knew exactly how Bilbo felt when he wished he were sitting in his favorite chair in front of a fire in his hobbit-hole, listening for the sound of his whistling kettle. That's where she'd rather be right now—home.

Greg and the tortoise were bobbing up ahead, waiting for her. As she finally caught up to them, a blue haze replaced the once bright light. The tortoise's diamonds shone like a ship's light through fog.

"Coming towards us is Gheir Island, where you will find your guide," the tortoise explained. "He will bring you to Keen, my home. Wait there for me." She turned her massive head to Amelia. "It is too dangerous for me to accompany you now. You must go on without me."

"What do you mean, too dangerous?" Greg asked.

"Hush, Gregory. Questions later. For now you must just do as I say."

Amelia hesitated. Should she tell the tortoise? Should she just blurt out, "I can't walk!" and explain that it would be impossible for her to get to Keen even with a guide? *Say something!* But she couldn't. The image of those fangs and eyes flashed through her mind. Without her chair, she'd have absolutely no chance of surviving if the monster came after her. At least Greg could run. She'd be the bait while he escaped.

"Amelia? Are you all right?" The tortoise nudged her arm, startling her out of her thoughts.

"Oh, yeah. I...um...I just..." *Say it. Say you can't walk.* "I'm fine."

"Yes, you are—absolutely fine."

Darkness was upon them. Chunks of dirt started plopping into the water around them. The island was directly overhead. Gheir Island was going to crush them!

"Get away, Amelia! Swim!" Greg grabbed her arm. Seawater poured into her mouth. She coughed and tried to suck air through her nose as Greg dragged her through the waves.

"Children, wait!" The tortoise's voice was firm. "First lesson... trust. Children, you must trust in order to learn how to survive on Mystic. Amelia, are you in danger?" The tortoise motioned to Amelia's chest. "Listen from within here." Then the tortoise nudged Amelia's head, sending drops of water running down her cheek. "Not from here."

Amelia gazed at the underside of the island. Panic raced through her veins. Her mind screamed *Danger!* But there was something else...a hint of a feeling inside her that she couldn't explain. A calm within the tension, like a tiny glowing seed trying to sprout.

"No." Amelia looked over at the tortoise, whose eyes were soft and comforting. Amelia's heart stopped racing and her breath slowed. "No, I don't think I'm in danger."

Greg spit out a mouthful of water. "Seriously?! Aaant—wrong answer! Go! Swim! Move, Mel! We're totally about to get crushed!" Greg pushed through the waves.

"Excellent, Amelia. If you are to survive on Mystic, you must listen with more than your ears and see with more than your eyes."

Greg stopped swimming and turned towards them. "What do you mean? Mel, what's she talking about? I just want to go home. How do we get home? C'mon, Mel, this is ridiculous! Look at that thing. Hurry!"

The island hovered over them for an instant, moved west, and dropped, crashing down into the Nimi Sea and sending a giant wave as tall as a skyscraper straight for them, rumbling terribly as it approached. Amelia braced herself.

Trust. The kind tortoise had said to trust. Amelia squeezed her eyes shut and felt the cool air on her face. *Trust.* Her body was scooped up and rocketed to the crest of the wave. She was sailing through the air, her body half under water and half peeking out from the tip of the wave. She had seconds of exhilaration and freedom—and then she was sucked down, the rush of the wave jetting over her head, pressure filling her ears. Down she went, but this time she was full of excitement. She opened her eyes and saw a rainbow of tiny fish swimming all around her, playing in her strands of floating hair. And she laughed.

Amelia swam back up to the surface, her head bursting from the water, fresh air filling her lungs. That was the most fun she'd had in a long time. A few feet away, Greg shook his head when he saw her. They swam to each other. She noticed his eyes were brighter blue than she remembered.

"We can be surfer dudes, eh?" Greg grinned. "We sure got lucky. What was with you back there? Did you believe all that crazy stuff about trust and think from here..."Greg pointed to her heart. "Not here." Greg pointed to his head.

She *did* believe it. Amelia searched for the right words.

"Hello? Mel?"

Amelia searched for the right words, but before she could spit out a reply, he shouted, "Look!"

Gheir Island sat majestically before them. Where once there was only sea, now there was land. Pristine white sand covered a beach as far as they could see to the east and west. Behind the beach stretched a canopy of lush green trees swaying as if they were waving hello. Paradise. They swam close to the shore. The tortoise faced them, her long black nails buried in the sand, her shell glistening. She rose up on her hind legs and extended her front legs.

"What's happening?" Greg whispered.

They watched as the tortoise morphed before their eyes, her sparkling black shell, wrinkled legs, and long accordion neck transforming into a curvy woman with flowing hair, dressed in an emerald-colored robe.

"Whoa!" Greg pointed. "Did you see that? She's a *woman*? A gorgeous woman!" Amelia splashed Greg for being so blunt.

"Hey!" Greg splashed her back.

"Gregory and Amelia, my name is Queen Fredonia. Welcome to Mystic."

CHAPTER 9

Greg was right. Queen Fredonia *was* beautiful. She was the most beautiful woman Amelia had ever seen; tall with an oval face, high cheekbones, deep dark eyes, and hair that cascaded down her shoulders in gentle waves all the way to her hips. Black jewels that once glistened on her shell now lined the sleeves and edges of her robe. Silver slippers hugged her feet. Greg didn't take his eyes off her. "Can you believe that?" he whispered. "Look at her."

Amelia felt the urge to splash him again, but didn't. She was too worried about what was coming next. She was going to have to crawl out of the water onto the sand.

Before either of them could speak, Queen Fredonia bid them farewell, waved her arms across her body, and disappeared.

"Where'd she go?" Greg hollered. "I thought she said our guide would be here waiting for us. I don't see anyone. Why would she leave us alone here? She knows it's not safe!" Greg swam towards the shore. He ran up unto the beach and yelled back at Amelia. "She's really gone! Now what?" He stopped and gazed down at his clothes.

"Ugh!" His wetsuit had changed shape to a robe and his sneakers were now slippers. "I look like a frickin' wizard or something. Hey, Queen Fredonia, the least you could have done was give me back my jeans and T-shirt!"

Amelia couldn't disagree. Her friend looked really Harry Potterish. Not his style. At all.

"I hate this robe!" Greg flung his arms around and called out down the beach. "Hello? Anybody out there? Queen Fredonia's friend—our guide... whatever you call yourself? We're here!" No one answered. "Great. So now what do we do?" Greg swiped his hand through his wet hair and shrugged. "I'm going to go see if I can find someone."

He started jogging down the beach. Good. She didn't want him to see her crawling out of the water. It wasn't going to be pretty. She pulled herself through the gentle waves until her knees hit sand. Water splashed onto her face, blending with the tears escaping from her eyes. Greg would never know she'd been crying. He'd obviously forgotten she couldn't walk. That was a mixed blessing. It meant he didn't see the wheelchair, he saw *her*. Just as he kept telling her he did. But it also meant she was stranded. Just watching Greg run up on shore was enough to make her envious. If only. He didn't know how lucky he was.

The blinding white sand was in sharp contrast to the dark forest beyond the shoreline. As she pulled herself onto the dry shore she noticed that her wetsuit had turned to a turquoise robe with sleeves just below her elbow and a high collar. Black diamonds lined the bottom edge. Silver slippers fit snugly on her feet. She took them off and flung them up the beach. What did she need slippers for? It didn't matter if the sand was hot. She wouldn't feel it.

Greg strolled along the water's edge, calling out for their guide. Between his shouts, Amelia could just make out soft music coming from the forest. It sounded like a flute.

She traced a diamond in the sand, then scooped it up and let it pour through her fingers—the sand was soft and smooth, like baking powder. If she closed her eyes, she could hardly tell the difference between the sand and the seawater. A flittering wing brushed against her cheek. Amelia turned. An insect with shimmering iridescent wings hovered in front of her face for an instant, then disappeared. "Wait!" she called after it. But it didn't return.

Amelia rolled over and pushed herself into a kneeling position. She might as well make her way towards the woods. If that was the direction to Keen, she was going to need a huge head start. But something was wrong.

Usually the weight of her legs would swing her hips too far to either side, but right now she was still, calm, perfectly balanced. Amelia felt the smoothness of the sand under her knees—cold and wet, like an ice pack. But no. She had no sensation in her legs—so she had to be imagining the cold, right? She flipped over and sat up. Sand stuck to her knees like paste. It *did* feel cold. She touched her foot. "Oh!" she gasped. She felt it! She ran her finger from her foot to her ankle and up to her knee. She felt it! She wasn't imagining anything.

Could it be possible? Amelia pushed the thought from her mind. It was too much to hope for. If she let herself believe... if she let herself take that risk, she would be crushed just like all those mornings in rehab when she'd woken up thinking, "Today's the day my legs are going to work." Crushed.

But what about the gash on Greg's forehead? It had disappeared. Could Mystic be different? Could she walk?

Amelia pinched herself below her left knee to make sure it was real. Yes! She felt the tight squeeze. "Oh my God!" She pinched her arm and then under her knee again. It was the same sensation. Pain—glorious pain! She felt jumpy and her mouth refused to stop smiling. She couldn't help it. *Please... please let me be able to walk.* Amelia's hands shook. *Try,* she urged herself. *At least try to stand.*

Amelia positioned her hands on either side of her right knee and bent her leg. She held it in place. Okay. Sand tickled the bottom of her foot and instinctively, she curled her toes. It was the greatest feeling ever! Her heart was beating so fast she knew there was no turning back. If she couldn't walk, her heart would explode into a billion pieces.

Amelia held her breath as she released the grip on her knee. Her leg stayed where it was. She exhaled. "Okay. Please stay," she muttered. She pulled her left leg back and up. Sand poured in between her toes. She wriggled her foot. "No way!" Amelia let go quickly. It stayed. She was sitting on the beach with her legs bent, toes in the sand. Had she ever been this happy in her life?

Amelia placed her hands behind her and leaned back. The shadow that had loomed inside her since the accident was bursting apart into specks of dust. *Don't try it—it'll hurt too much if it doesn't work.* But, to walk again... why was she even allowing herself to think of the possibility?

Trust.

She tightened her abdomen and placed her hands at her sides. She closed her eyes, focusing on the soothing music still coming from the forest. She imagined herself flying, then landing, running, splashing along the shore. *Do it...try!*

Amelia opened her eyes and let out a cry of exhilaration. *Go!* She pushed down, rocked forward, and squeezed her leg muscles. They burst with energy. She forced her feet into the sand and—stood up! "Oh my god!"

Her legs felt foreign, like they didn't belong to her. But they did, they were her legs, her standing legs! And she was taller. So much taller! *Thank you! Thank you!* She watched the light dance across the Nimi Sea. She was healed. Mystic was magical.

A wave crashed on shore and crept towards her toes. She wiggled them again. Losing her balance for a moment, she thrust her arms out like the wings of an airplane. She balanced, then tipped a little too far to the right and down she went. She laughed and laughed.

"Mel? What's going on?" Greg was by her side, looking panicked.

"Did you see me?" She was still laughing. "Did you see?"

"Yes...I...How did you...You can walk? Can you do it again?" Greg braced her arm to help her. She resisted.

"It's okay, I can do it."

Greg nodded and stepped back. She pushed off the sand. It was easier this time. Her legs jiggled like jelly, making her laugh harder. Yes!

"Wow! Look at you, Mel! I'd hug you... but I'm afraid I'd knock you over. This is awesome!"

This is just what she'd wished for that day at Greg's locker. The two of them face to face. She stared back at him, feeling something she'd never felt before. Total awkwardness with a sprinkle of...like. Not *like* as a best friend but *like* as a boyfriend. Amelia rubbed her sweaty palms down her robe.

"Well, are you going to walk, or what?" Greg took a step towards her, offering his hand.

"I don't know..."Amelia shrugged. Walk. She used to do it effortlessly, without thinking. Now it was the most important thing to her in the world. *Take his hand.*

"C'mon...you can do it... grab my hands."

Amelia shook her head. "It's okay, let me try it myself."

"You can do it, Amelia. I know you can."

The sand was a soft blanket to cushion her fall. If she fell, she'd get right back up and try again. It was as simple as that. Right?

Slowly Amelia lifted her right leg. Her hands flew out to her sides. She placed her foot down just a few inches in front of her.

"Good job," Greg whispered.

Amelia placed all her weight on her right leg and raised her left foot.

"Look!" She balanced on one foot for a moment. "Greg, can you believe this?" He shook his head. Tears rolled down his cheeks.

Amelia leaned back and put her foot down. "Wooo-hooooo!"

She was herself again. It all came rushing back. Amelia took three self-assured steps and then kicked the water, splashing Greg.

"Hey!" He laughed and wiped his face. "I can't believe it. You're amazing."

Amelia rubbed her legs. "Thank you!" She twirled around, despite being still a little wobbly, and let out another squeal of pleasure. "Thank you!"

Suddenly she felt herself being lifted from behind. Greg was stronger than she'd thought. She kicked her legs and yelled, pretending she wanted him to put her down. Greg's breath was tickling her neck. She placed her hands on top of his. Her stomach felt all tingly.

"You're my hero!" He twirled her around and around and finally placed her gently on the sand... on her feet. The trees, sand, and water were circled around her. "No more wheels, Mel."

She felt the awkwardness again, and glanced down. He touched a water droplet under her eye and guided it down her cheek to her chin, lifting her face to meet his. His eyes were shiny with tears.

"No more wheels," she repeated. Chills trembled through her body even though the air was warm. This was Greg; goofy, sarcastic Greg, her football buddy. *Football!* Amelia let go of Greg's hand. "Find a football... okay, a coconut or something, and let's play!"

She ran up the beach towards the forest, her legs strengthening with each step. Greg chased her. The music in the trees grew louder. It had a Celtic feel to it that made her want to dance a jig and kick up her feet right there on the beach; she didn't care if she looked a fool. She didn't care about anything. Amelia jumped into the air, raised her arms, and shouted, "I'm free!"

"Gotcha!" His arms were around her waist right before she hit the sand. He tackled her! She spit sand and rolled onto her side. Greg laughed.

"You said you wanted to play football. Oh, I'm sorry, didn't you have the ball? I thought you were heading into the woods for a touchdown." Greg lay on his side, elbow in the sand, hand propping up his head.

Amelia sat up and wiped her mouth. "Brat!" She swiped the sand from her robe. This new freedom to sit or stand…she wasn't stuck anymore. "I'm me again." Saying the words out loud brought forth a burst of tears that made her body quiver. She covered her face.

Greg pulled her close to him. "You always were you, Mel. Sitting, standing… you're the same cool girl I've known for years. I have to say, though… I'm going to miss calling you Crip." He lowered her hands, pushed on her nose gently, and put his arm around her.

Amelia couldn't speak. Sparks were igniting inside her, but on the outside she was frozen. He was definitely flirting with her and her emotions were all tangled up like a ball of rubber bands. Maybe she should bounce up and challenge him to a race. She felt his breath on her cheeks and closed her eyes when she saw him lean in closer to her.

CHAPTER 10

Snap!

They bumped foreheads as they turned to see what was behind them. Greg leapt to his feet.

Snap!

Amelia rose and stepped back. Flashes of the monster came rushing to her mind. Greg held his hands out, guarding her.

Snap!

"Greg, let's get out of here," Amelia whispered.

But before they could move, a deep voice echoed through a bramble of bushes, "Dear me, there you are! I'm coming...I'm coming! I've been waiting for you for hours! I drifted off to sleep and suddenly I was awakened by screams!"

A strange hairy creature barreled through the bushes. He strode towards them on thick legs, a long tail leaving a trail in the sand behind him. Amelia, too shocked to move, couldn't figure out if he was a lion or a man. He kept rambling on about waiting for them, but Amelia couldn't take her eyes off his sharp black claws that tapped the outside of a book he carried under his massive forearm. Greg kept his hands out to shield Amelia. Amelia was glad for the gesture, but who was he kidding? Greg was puny next to this enormous lion-man.

He stopped in front of them, beads of sweat cascading down his mane onto the sand. That's when it occurred to her that she shouldn't have stayed still in fascination; she should have run away! Now he could kill both of them with one swish of his tail, which looked alarmingly like a weapon with a shiny spiked ball attached to the end of it. One hard knock in the head and they'd be goners. Circling, the creature inspected them up and down.

"It is most unpleasant to be awakened in such a manner! Imagine my distress when I realized it was you. And trouble seems to follow you wherever you go, child... I mean..." He cleared his throat, stepped around Greg, and bent down towards Amelia. "And just why were you convulsing so, and why was this young man chasing you? Are you in need of some assistance, or are you just a tad loony?"

"I'm not loony," she announced firmly. "I'm just really, really happy. That's why I was kicking my feet, screaming, and spinning around in circles. You see ... I can walk, and I haven't been able to walk since..."

The creature had begun to flip through his book, totally ignoring her. Amelia waved her hands to get his attention, but it was no use. "Greg and I were just celebrating." Amelia touched Greg's shoulder and nodded. They started to run towards the water.

"Excuse me, Amelia, child, but you should definitely not go off unprotected!" The creature's bass voice vibrated through her body. "Please come back here at once. I must insist." Before she had a chance to decide whether she would listen, Amelia found her legs carrying her back to him, with Greg right behind her. Strange. They stood in front of the lion and waited for him to lower his book.

"Hey!" Greg furrowed his brow and crossed his arms, trying to look tough. "How did you know her name? Who are you anyway?"

Amelia nodded and tried to look as serious as Greg. As happy as she was, she needed to focus, calm down, and figure out who this lion-man was. But just as she'd known instinctively that Gheir Island wasn't going to land on them, she knew this blustery lion-man was totally harmless.

"Oh, how rude. My apologies. I am Winston, your guide, a curler from Ice Hills."

"Winston, it is nice to meet you. I am Amelia and this is Greg. From Pennsylvania." Amelia held out her hand. He took it and gently gave it a shake. His palms felt leathery like the bottom of a cat's paw and his clawed fingers extended far beyond her wrist. One squeeze and he could have broken all the bones in her hand. But his shiny black eyes and long amber lashes reminded her suddenly of the big cuddly bear she'd won for Joey at the E-town fair last summer.

Winston motioned towards Greg who shook his hand quickly and lowered his head. Then Winston noticed Amelia's slippers lying in the sand, picked them up, and tossed them to her. "Amelia, child, we are heading into the forest. You will need these." She giggled as she balanced on one leg at a time and slipped them on. She nodded at Greg as if to say, "Did you see that?"

"Impressive."

Winston held up his book. "Queen Fredonia lent me her book so I could study your world. I've been reading all about your Earth in this *Book of Time*. Very unusual, your world." Winston placed his hand on her shoulder. "Amelia, I'm overjoyed to see you're walking again. Isn't Mystic wondrous? It's quite powerful, and you will find you can do many things here in Mystic that you cannot on Earth. How was the Nimi Sea? Marvelous with all its colors, yes? It says here even though Earth has many oceans, humans can't breathe underwater. Too bad. Maybe one day your species will evolve. The Nimi Sea must have been shocking for you, to say the least. Yes, Mystic is a marvelous world. My favorite. Well, I suppose it should be since I'm from Ice Hills. There's no place like home." Winston winked at her.

"Wait, wait, *wait* just a second!" Greg spluttered. "*You're* our guide? You're the one that's supposed to take us to Keen?" Greg began to pace, kicking up sand. "Can you *please* just tell us how we can get back home? I mean *our* home?"

Home. Winston's words echoed in Amelia's mind. Was Winston saying she could only walk while in Mystic? When she got home, would she have to return to her wheelchair—is that what he meant? Amelia plopped down in the sand. She felt sick. She couldn't go back to the wheelchair. She wouldn't. No way. She was never going back to that life again.

But what about Greg? What if Grandma K. had survived? And Ms. Linda? And Joey? How could she leave Joey? She promised him she'd be back. No! Then there was E-town. Elizabethtown—cows grazing in the hills, corn stalks swaying in the breeze, and roads climbing and dropping like rollercoaster tracks. She loved knowing that whenever she smelled the delicious scent of melting chocolate from the candy factory, it was going to rain. She loved the way people greeted each other in the supermarket. She loved quiet evenings sitting on the porch listening to the neighborhood kids chase fireflies. She loved knowing that every day at twelve o'clock the church bells would chime. *Home.*

But...they'd all eventually understand that walking was more important than anything. Wouldn't they? Amelia gazed over at Winston and Greg. They'd stopped talking to watch her.

"Amelia, child, are you all right?"

"I *can't* go home, Greg," she whispered.

"What do you mean you can't go home, Mel? Of *course* we're going home. As soon as we get to Keen, the Queen will show us how to get back to E-town—back to our lives..." Greg glared at Winston. "On Earth."

Amelia's eyes met Greg's for an instant, then darted to Winston. "Winston said I'm healed while I'm in Mystic. If I go back..."

"I'm sure that's not what he meant. Right, Winston? She'll still be able to walk when we go home, won't she?"

Winston shook his huge head.

Taking Amelia's hand, Greg tried to help her up, but she stayed down on the sand. "You *have* to come home, Mel. I've already lost Grandma K. I can't lose you too. Please, Amelia..."

"Do you realize what you're asking me to do?" She wriggled her hands back under the sand. "I...can't."

The decision was made. No more wheelchair. But Greg didn't understand. How could he? "Greg, maybe there's a reason we're here. Both of us I mean. Maybe we're not *supposed* to leave."

"Elizabethtown is our home, not Mystic. What if Winston's wrong? You can't know for sure unless you go back."

"Yeah, and if I go back and I'm still paralyzed...then what?"

Winston continued to shake his head. "He knows, Greg." Amelia paused. "I'll help you get home...but I'm not going with you." Her voice was flat and direct.

Greg turned his back to her and walked towards Winston. "And what if this place turns out to be horrible, Mel? Even if you hate it, you're still going to stay just because you can walk?"

56

"Yes."

But…could she really face never seeing him again?

"Come along, children." Winston's booming voice interrupted her thoughts. "We must get to Keen. We should be safe there until Queen Fredonia returns."

"Should be safe. Safe from what? I don't understand why we're in danger in the first place." Greg motioned for Winston to take the lead, but he refused to look at Amelia. "Never mind. Forget it. Let's just go."

Amelia pushed herself up, kicked the sand, then lifted each knee into the air as if she were marching. Her legs astounded her. Why couldn't Greg be happy for her?

Winston led them along the path he'd created through the woods. Sounds of Winston's large feet crunching sticks masked the beautiful flute music Amelia had heard earlier. Images of Greg spinning her in circles played through her mind. Greg was hurting, and as much as she wished she could put that out of her mind, she couldn't.

Crunch, swish, snap. The forest was dense, light barely trickling down through the leaves, making it difficult for Amelia to see more than a foot around her. She'd been counting her footsteps, but lost track after three thousand four hundred fifty something.

She could hear Greg's steps far behind. He hated her now, and she didn't blame him. He was the loyal one. She was not. That's probably why her Ayer didn't have a wolf on it. She wasn't a loyal friend. Amelia bent down to pinch her leg. It hurt. Good. Some things were more important than friendship. Still, she couldn't shake the eerie feeling that loomed like a dark shadow and was growing inside her. It was a heaviness that made her want to lie down and go to sleep.

"I sense you feel it too." Winston passed her the book and snapped a large branch that blocked their way. He tossed the pieces into the bushes, then motioned for Greg to catch up.

"What are you talking about? I'm fine, Winston. Are we almost there?"

"Amelia, you must listen to your instincts, child. It takes skill to listen carefully. Clear your mind of all thought, and feel what's inside you—peace, unrest, or danger?"

She felt like she'd just been caught daydreaming in school. Why wouldn't he just leave her alone? Did he really need to lecture her right now? She wasn't in the mood.

Greg jogged up to them. "What's wrong? Why'd we stop?"

Suddenly, Amelia knew. She felt an intense darkness that cut to her bones. *Danger!* Something was out there. She couldn't see it; but she could feel it, just like Winston had said.

Wind whooshed through the tree canopies. And then Amelia heard the whipping sound of flapping wings. "It's coming!" she screamed.

Her Ayer lit up, and she saw the yellow-eyed monster lowering from the sky. Coming right towards Greg.

"Greg, look out!" Amelia ran towards him, but suddenly Winston's massive arm was around her waist, pulling her backwards.

"Let me go! Let me go!"

Winston covered her mouth with his paw-like hand and shot into the air. They flew over and under branches, zooming through the darkness. Her feet slammed into a branch, and pain shot up her legs. She grasped Winston's fur, clutching as tightly as she could.

They had to go back for Greg. They had to!

Winston dove, Amelia now upside down in his arms. They were heading straight for the ground. She was going to be sick. *Please... please...* She shut her eyes and held her breath, trying to keep her stomach from shooting out her mouth. Then they stopped so quickly, she couldn't tell if she was upside down or right side up. She staggered, let go of Winston, and lowered herself to the ground. She was alive! Now, if she could just stop spinning. Winston seemed to be mumbling. What was he saying?

"Geupchil."

Amelia rested her head on her arms. Greg...*Where are you?* She couldn't move. She felt herself being raised into the air once more. "Hey!"

"Hush, child. We have to go inside." Winston started to mumble again. Her mind was still spinning and her body wobbled like a marionette.

Winston carried her to a huge rock, then led her under some thick branches into a dark entryway next to the rock.

"Greg?" Her voice was weak.

"Hush, child."

They were in a cave. In complete darkness. They were safe. Winston had saved her. But where was Greg? Why had Winston left him in the forest to face the monster alone?

Drip. Water was dripping somewhere. *Drip*—her best friend was gone. *Drip*—it was her fault. *Drip*—she never should've told Greg she wasn't going back home.

CHAPTER 11

L ights blinked from the cave's ceiling like the fluorescent bulbs at school that flickered on one by one across a classroom.

"We are safe now," Winston said, walking over to the wall.

Amelia ran her hands up and down her legs to try and stop the trembling. Her mind was a jumbled mess. *Focus.* She looked around. Where were they? The pale peach-colored stone walls were covered with drawings: animals, people, creatures, villages, and strange circular symbols. The illustrations reminded her of hieroglyphics.

"Lovely, aren't they? Walterboros are such talented artists." Winston ran his hand along some of the images. "This one is my favorite. It's a picture of our market where nus and wizards used to gather, trade goods, and celebrate the day. Look at all the smiles..." His voice dropped. "That was before Ralient began destroying our villages."

"What?" What was he talking about? Amelia marched over to Winston. "Where's Greg? Why did you leave him?"

Winston shook his head. Amelia ran back to the rock that now blocked the cave's entrance. "Open it!"

"Greg is gone, child —taken like so many others. There was nothing I could do for him. I had to protect *you*." Winston had his back to her, continuing to run his hands along the wall like he was searching for something.

"We *have* to go back!" Amelia pushed hard against the rock, trying to slide it away from the entrance. "Now!"

"Oh, no, that's completely out of the question. And the rock isn't going to budge, child. Don't waste your energy."

"Open it, Winston. You're strong enough. Open it now!"

"Amelia, child, the Walterboros have locked us in for the night. Even I cannot make the rock move. You should be grateful they have allowed us refuge."

"Grateful? Are you kidding?" Amelia slid down to the dirt floor. She covered her face with her hands and sobbed. Why had she been so mean to her best friend? Why hadn't she just let him believe she would return home with him?

Winston settled his great bulk next to her. Sweat glistened on his fur, and the smell reminded her of a dog after a bath. He waited for a while then said, "Greg was taken by a Khala, my dear. There is nothing we can do to help him right now. So, up you get and stop your blubbering. I've found the secret passage to the Great Hall. We will eat, sleep, and when light comes tomorrow, we will continue on our way to Keen." Winston stood, holding out his hand to her.

Amelia sniffed. "A Khala! What's that? Why does it want Greg? And don't treat me like a two-year-old!" The words spilled out of her like blood pouring from a wound. There was no stopping them. "I've been sucked up in a red light, spit out into the sea, saved by a talking turtle who's really a Queen, discover I'm in a totally different world—and now my best friend's been abducted! I think I've got every right to cry or scream or whatever right now!"

She took a deep breath. And suddenly she felt very tiny sitting there on the cold damp Earth. Winston looked at her, showing no emotion. Amelia slid her legs to her chest and wrapped her arms around her knees. Water dripped. Winston waited. Amelia pressed her back against the rock and then stood up, not taking her eyes off the lion-man.

Winston cleared his throat and bowed. "My apologies, child. I should not have been so rude."

That's it? That's all he was going to say after she screamed at him? He could've squashed her, thrown her across the room, slapped her, something...

Too embarrassed to apologize, she said, "Winston, please just tell me what really happened back there."

"The danger you felt in the forest was real, child. A *Khala* was watching us—waiting for the right moment to strike. We are fortunate there was only one. Usually they travel in gangs of four or five. Khalas are fierce winged creatures with hollow yellow eyes and fangs. Their claws can tear..." Winston whacked the dirt floor with his tail. "Well, let's just say their claws are very sharp indeed."

Amelia felt a fierce burning in her throat. The creature she'd seen on the windshield before they crashed—it was a Khala! Something like *that* was after Greg? It didn't make any sense. What had a creature from Mystic been doing on Earth?

Winston guided her to a cave painting. "See as the Walterboros have seen. Look. Mystic is changing, and the reality that once was has ended. It is the Khalas' darkness that you are still feeling now—left over from the forest. It's contagious, like a sickness. May I suggest changing your thoughts to something that brings you joy? It will help ease your fearful mind."

Amelia gazed at the painting. "What the—?" she gasped. Every detail was exact...It was her bedroom at home! Her bed and *The Hobbit* on her nightstand, and she was sitting in front of her computer! There, staring in her bedroom window were those yellow eyes. A Khala.

Amelia ran her palm across the image. "That thing...that monster's been watching me? I don't understand, Winston. Why's a Khala after me? What does it want?"

Winston didn't reply, but pushed on the image of *The Hobbit*. With a creak and scrape, the entire wall opened up to reveal two long, dimly-lit passageways.

"I'm not entirely sure," Winston said, shrugging. "Perhaps you possess something the Khala wants."

"Oh, like some sort of ring of invisibility or something? That's the craziest thing I've ever heard. I have nothing some monster like that would want!"

Ignoring Amelia's outburst, Winston directed them down a passage to the right. Suddenly his fur rose like that of a frightened cat. Amelia stopped. Winston turned to her. "Oh, dear me! I left the *Book of Time* in the forest! When I scooped you up, I must have dropped it." Winston muttered something else and then started to lope down the path.

"Wait!" she called. But Winston was faster than she'd expected, and she had to run to catch up to him. When she finally reached him, he was tapping his claws together as he walked. More lights flickered, illuminating more drawings. "Winston, please tell me, why's the Khala after *me?*"

"No worries, no worries, we can go out at first light to retrieve the book. I know where I must have dropped it. We'll recover the book and then head straight for Keen. This is most interesting indeed." His fur settled back into place. "I believe the Great Hall is just down this way. Oh, some lime juice is exactly what we need." Winston licked his lips. "Wait until you try their sweet berries and cream…Walterboros are exquisite chefs."

Amelia had to jog to keep up. She leaped over his tail every time it came too close to her legs. "Winston, you aren't making any sense. Just… why won't you answer my question?"

"And it is a very good question, child. But not one to which *I* can give you the answer right now. If Queen Fredonia permits us, we will look for your friend."

"*Permits* us?" Amelia stopped. "I don't need permission to find Greg. We *have* to help him. He could die! What's wrong with you?"

She was going to find Greg no matter what, even if she had to go alone. Winston had answers, but was refusing to tell her. She was walking…and still trapped.

Winston swung his body around so fast it startled her. "I believe your first lesson from Queen Fredonia was to *trust*, was it not?" He continued down the passage.

How could she trust everything would be okay now? Trust. It was easy for him to say. His friend hadn't been kidnapped by a Khala.

Her slippers shuffled on the damp dirt as they walked, and then a glimmering light caught her attention. She paused. Tiny black diamonds shone around a full-length mirror set into the stone wall. Amelia stared at her reflection; a girl standing, in a turquoise robe, straggly windblown hair and narrow, worried eyes. Winston loomed behind her. "Walterboros are quite hospitable. They have prepared a feast for us. Come see." ·

The drawings on the walls were eerie—as though they were watching her every step. Like teachers standing guard in the hallways, waiting for students to slip up and sneak a kiss or take out a cell phone. Every few seconds, she'd whip her head around to catch a glimpse of movement, but saw nothing.

What were these Walterboro creatures, and how the heck did they know what her bedroom looked like, for them to draw it? Were they spying on her, too?

The sweet aroma of freshly baked cookies wafted through the air. Amelia's stomach gurgled. What kind of friend would she be, eating while Greg was missing, probably scared, alone, and starving? If he was even still alive... The tornado in her mind made her dizzy.

"Still your mind, child. There's nothing we can do except eat and sleep, and that's what we shall do now. Hmmm. Hmmm." Winston began humming, a noise that sounded almost like a purr.

Amelia felt something behind her and spun around. Nothing.

"They're quick," Winston said with a chuckle. "I doubt you'll ever see one. Walterboros are also known for their magnificent liquid creations. Lime juice, berry squish twist, swirly bubbly, and jumpin' gigglies. I wonder which they have made for us tonight. Hmmm, hmmm, hmmm."

Winston's purring resonated off the stone. Walterboros again. "Winston, what *is* a Walterboro? Some sort of ghost?"

"Oh, no, child, they are very much alive. They're highly intelligent beings with jolly plump bodies, warm eyes, and cute black noses that twitch when they speak. They are quite shy and extremely sensitive, so please choose your words carefully if ever you are lucky enough to speak to one. You don't want to insult them or hurt their feelings. According to the *Book of Time,* you have a similar creature on Earth. They're called...*rats*. Only in Mystic, they are much bigger—about your height. Maybe taller?" Winston raised his hand above Amelia's head. "Yes, perhaps closer to six feet tall."

"*What?* Rats! Are you teasing me?" She shuddered.

"No, I rarely tease, child. I'm not even a hundred percent sure what teasing is."

"Joking, kidding...pulling my leg."

"Pulling your leg? I don't see what that has to do with joking, which is like..."

"Never mind, Winston."

Giant rats? Yikes! Hopefully "shy" meant they'd stay hidden and far away in a corner somewhere. Continuously glancing around, Amelia tiptoed behind Winston, continuing through a series of connecting tunnels. Lights blinked on as they passed, illuminating their way. She had to allow herself to trust Winston. A little, anyway.

Winston had a big grin on his face. "Ahh, yes, just as I thought. They have prepared a feast for us. We are most grateful!" Winston called out. No one answered. Thank goodness.

They stood in a large, ornately decorated, circular room. The soft strumming music resonated quietly throughout the chamber. Giant wooden chairs surrounded a long, rectangular wooden table, perfect for Winston's mammoth size. She was three sizes too small to fit in any of them. She felt like Goldilocks.

"Sit, child, let's eat." Winston motioned for her to sit down. Then he extended his hands under water that ran from a fountain centerpiece. He splashed water across his face, spraying droplets everywhere. Tiny blue flowers decorated the base of the fountain. Winston picked the smallest one and handed it to Amelia. "Beautiful, isn't it?"

Amelia nodded and examined the flower. It was just a flower. What was she supposed to do with it?

"*Look*, child. Notice the flower, the table, everything in this room at this very moment. You are so lost in your mind, you cannot appreciate all the gifts that are before you now." Winston took a seat at the far end of the table.

It was as though he could read her mind. Amelia twirled the flower between her fingers and then rubbed it along her cheek like she used to do with the satin part of her baby blanket. It brought back a memory of her imaginary friend, Coral, singing to her as she tried to fall asleep in one of her new foster homes.

"Eat, child." Winston shook his head at her.

Amelia climbed into a chair. Her feet dangled, and she kicked them simply because she could.

In front of her stood a bowl of silver and copper berries and a tall green drinking glass topped with a foamy rainbow made of bubbles. One by one, each bubble popped and another rose out of the glass to take its place. She flicked one of the bubbles, which drifted towards Winston, landing in his leathery palm. "Delicious! Lime juice. Give it a try, Amelia."

Amelia shivered, imagining rats preparing her meal.

"Just eat, child." Winston frowned. He read her well.

Amelia sank her spoon deep into a bowl of berries that looked more like marbles. Squishy marbles... Quickly, she shoved the spoon past her chapped lips and into her mouth. A burst of sweetness exploded on her tongue. Better than mint chocolate chip ice cream, her absolute favorite. This was the most incredible tasting berry she'd ever had. Amelia didn't stop eating to talk or even to glance in Winston's direction. When she was done, she ran her finger along the edge of the bowl wondering if she could fit more into her already bursting stomach.

"Good? Now try the lime juice." Winston's face was soft in the dim light. Despite his bluntness, he was kind. And he had the best manners of anyone she'd ever met.

Amelia picked up her glass and sipped. The tart juice sizzled in her mouth, then went down like a thick hot chocolate. Amelia could've had more of the delicious liquid, but her eyes were fighting to close, and her mind couldn't hold on to a single thought. She needed to sleep.

A tingling on her arm caught her attention. The blue bead on her Ayer was shining brighter than the others. Electric blue, the color of Greg's eyes. Her heart hurt, she missed him so much. He would've loved this meal, she thought dreamily.

CHAPTER 12

"Up you get, up you get, child. It's first light and we must go." Her eyes blinked open. Fabric squeezed tightly around her. She was a cocoon lying on the dirt floor.

"Where...where am I?" Amelia wiggled her arms free and sat up.

"You are on the floor." Winston held out a glass of lime juice. Was that his attempt at humor? Last she remembered she had been sitting at a table eating dinner. "You're in the Walterboros' sleeping chambers. Look at the drawings, they're—"

"Magnificent?" Amelia interrupted.

"You sound so much better, child. I'm glad to see a rest has done you good. Now, look above you."

"Oh!" Amelia whispered. The ceiling was like a planetarium with stars and planets and galaxies stretching from one end of the room to the other. "It's beautiful." Winston pulled her to her feet and handed her the lime juice. She stepped out of the tangle of blankets. "Thank you, Winston."

"You are most welcome, child. Happy to see your eyes back to their beautiful brightness."

Amelia watched as the rainbow bubbles from the lime juice twinkled like the stars surrounding them.

Winston nodded. Then he picked up the blankets, folding them precisely, making sure all sides were exactly even, and set them against the wall. "Drink up."

A bubble popped on her nose. Laughing, she caught the next one in her mouth, then finished her juice and set the glass next to the blankets. "Hey, wait for me!" she called.

Winston was striding down the cave's path at a quick pace. She ran after him. Winston's long tail left a zigzag pattern in the dirt. Pausing a moment to look at his cat-like tracks, Amelia noticed a particular drawing on the wall. "Winston! Look!" But he was gone.

The drawing depicted Queen Fredonia. But she wasn't in Mystic. She was in a room with a picture of Albert Einstein with his tongue sticking out and silver dollars scattered across a bureau—it was Grandma K.'s bedroom! "No way!" The Queen...with Grandma K. standing there in her Phillies cap, librarian glasses, and *Because I can* T-shirt.

Amelia took off running. "Winston! Winston!"

"Not so loud child, you'll disturb the Walterboros." Winston waited at the cave entrance. The rock had moved aside and bright light streamed through, making his mane look like a halo.

"Winston, come see... uh... just hurry!" Amelia clutched her stomach, panting. "Grandma K.!..."

"Hmmm, yes, come along, we mustn't dilly dally."

"Winston! Maybe there's a clue that will help us find Greg! How do the Walterboros know about Grandma K.? This... the Walterboros are trying to help us. I'm sure of it! Please!" Winston wasn't budging. What was the matter with him?

"Are all young ladies on Earth so stubborn? We must find the *Book of Time*. Gheir Island does not stay in one place for long—it is too dangerous. We have to get to Keen."

"Winston... but... forget it. *I'm* going back."

Amelia knew Winston was following her. She could hear the shuffle of his giant feet behind her. *Good!*

Suddenly, bristly fur brushed against her cheek. "Put me down!"

And then they were flying outside, Amelia tucked into Winston's deep armpit.

"Hey!" Cold air stung her squinted eyes. *How dare he!* She kicked and yelled, but it made no difference.

"Really now. Stop making such a fuss. I hope Queen Fredonia's right about you, because you certainly are testing my patience. Such abominable behavior."

"What'd you say?" Amelia spit a clump of fur out of her mouth. "Put me down! I can walk! Let me walk!"

"No. Amelia, look at the beauty of Gheir Island; the sand, the forest, and the white sky. Trust that you are exactly where you should be." Winston dodged under and over branches as he soared.

"When Greg's safe, I'll relax," Amelia said. "If you're not going to take us back to the cave, then take me to where he was kidnapped. Maybe we'll find some kind of trail." *A trail? How can I track a flying Khala? What a dumb idea.*

"Wonderful idea! That's precisely where we're going." And without warning, Winston bolted towards the ground.

"Winston!" *And he thinks I'm loony?* The lime juice swished in her gut.

"There it is. I see it. Hold on!" Winston banked to the left and landed in a patch of berries. He lowered her to the ground and kept a tight grip while she steadied herself.

"Never again! I mean it! Who taught you to fly anyway, Winston? You almost killed us!"

"I highly doubt that, child. Where's your sense of adventure?"

"It's between the pages of a book!"

Winston shook his mane. Berries went flying.

This was the exact spot where they'd last seen Greg. Amelia spun around. She swore she saw movement among some trees behind them. "Winston, did you see that?"

"Your imagination, child. The *Book of Time* is here somewhere. Hmmm." Winston brushed his arm across the bushes, pushing all the leaves aside with one swoop.

Amelia peered into the forest, her mind flashing back to the moments before Greg was taken. Queen Fredonia had said to trust. The Ayer was fine—no bright lights. But she was feeling...something...

"Winston, I don't get how to use this Ayer. What do all these beads do?" Amelia twisted it around on her wrist.

"You will find out soon enough, child. It's best if you leave it alone for now."

Amelia rolled her eyes. "Fine." She picked a leaf off a low branch. Why had the Khala taken Greg? The drawing in the Walterboros' cave showed the Khala watching *her*—not Greg.

"The Khala is after *you*." Winston blurted it out as if he'd been listening to her thoughts.

"What?" Amelia dropped the leaf.

"The Khala wants *you*, child. It took Greg, knowing you would try to save him. It's a trap."

"Why didn't you tell me before?"

"What did you feel in here?" Winston pointed to her gut.

"This is ridiculous. Why do you keep telling me to trust...trust that you are exactly where you should be...trust that Greg is okay...Winston, how can I trust when everything's gone so wrong?"

"Has *everything* gone wrong, child?" Winston was looking at her legs. "You are more than you know. More than you will let yourself believe. What you see in front of you...is it real or imagined?"

"What are you talking about? Of course it's real."

"If we were on Earth and I told you about a place called Mystic, where you could run free, would you have believed me or said it was imaginary? Yet, here you are." Winston tapped her forehead. "Think, child, what happened to you that day in the woods on Poplar Lane?"

Winston's eyes grew wide. Amelia hesitated. "Winston, what is it?"

He sprang to a pile of leaves behind her and rummaged through them. "There you are!" He picked up the *Book of Time* and brushed the dirt from its tattered cover.

"Now, child, we must journey to Keen and see if Quee....."

"Not so fast, Curler!" squealed a voice behind them. "Put the book down!"

CHAPTER 13

Peeking out from behind a crooked tree was a half-naked, scrawny, long-haired boy with a bow stretched back, aimed right at Winston. Surely this little kid didn't really think he could stand up to Winston and win, did he?

"I beg your pardon, young man, but this is Queen Fredonia's book, and I must return it to her promptly! We don't have time for explanations, so put that arrow back in its quiver where it belongs, and be on your way."

The bow and arrow shook terribly in the boy's trembling hands, but his voice was foolishly strong. This was turning out to be quite a show.

"It's really okay, little boy," Amelia hastened to explain. "Winston's telling the truth. He dropped this book last night when a—"

"Rotten human." The strange boy spat at her. "Stay out of this, or I will shoot you first!"

"What did you just call me?" Amelia baited him. "You shoot one of those at me and I'll come over there and snap them all in half before you can say hot fudge sundae—which obviously you should be eating more of!"

A loud croaking echoed suddenly through the trees.

Amelia jumped. Winston snorted and covered his mouth. "I found that humorous, child. I'm sorry if my laughter startled you."

Laughter? "Sheesh." Amelia muttered. She glanced back just in time to see an arrow headed right for her face. *Crap!*

Like a frog snatching a fly, Winston reached out and caught the white arrow just an inch from Amelia's nose. He crushed it in his paw, his claws glistening in the light. The slivers of wood sprinkled to the forest floor and disappeared among the leaves and dirt.

Silence.

"You will apologize for your rudeness, boy!"

"I'm...I'm sorry."

"Does Queen Fredonia know you are trespassing on her land?" Sticks crunched under Winston's big feet like brittle bones as he marched towards the boy.

The boy took a step back and made to grab another arrow. His hands were trembling so badly, he couldn't get a grip on a single one.

"No you don't," Winston growled.

"It's okay, Winston," Amelia said. "I'm fine. Let's leave him alone."

"He tried to kill you, Amelia!" Winston roared. "I will take care of this!"

Amelia ran to Winston, staying clear of his tail, which was ready to strike. "No! Stop, Winston! I'm okay! He's just a boy..."

"Who are you, boy?" Winston thundered.

"I... uh... I am Meesha...from Volarit."

"And why are you here?" Winston leaned way over the boy, making him cower.

"Winston, that's enough!" Amelia grabbed his arm.

"My village was attacked. A Khala dropped me here. Now I am trying to find Queen Fredonia to ask her to help my village."

"And your family?"

Meesha said nothing. Winston studied the boy. "A Khala dropped you here, you say? That is most interesting."

Amelia knew Meesha was lying about the Khala. He had to be. There wasn't a scratch on him. She felt a tinge of sadness for him. He looked so desperate and...scared.

"Come on, Winston," she urged. "Let's go—leave him. He's not going to hurt us now."

"Meesha," Winston announced, his voice only a shade softer, "is coming with us."

"What?" Meesha and Amelia asked in unison.

"Meesha of Volarit, this is Amelia."

She didn't want Winston to hurt the kid, but she also didn't want him tagging along. "He can't come with us!"

Winston ignored her and, with the *Book of Time* securely under his arm, began clearing a path. Now Meesha was smirking. Brat! She never should've felt sorry for him.

"Come along. We will hike to Keen." Winston waved to Amelia to follow. She didn't. Meesha did.

He was taller than she'd originally thought—almost her height. His black hair draped down over his shoulders. *He looks like a mangy Mowgli.*

"Must I carry you, Amelia? I'd rather not, but I will…"

Amelia sighed. "Fine… I'm coming. I just want to take one last look around the tree where Greg was taken—maybe I'll find something."

Winston nodded and started walking with Meesha.

Amelia crouched down by the tree. Two indentations in the dirt caught her eye. Greg's footprints!. "I'm going to find you, Greg," she whispered. "I promise."

CHAPTER 14

Amelia shuffled along the path, shoving branches away from her face and listening to Winston's low humming wafting on the breeze.

Meesha fell behind. He was busy sharpening his arrows, and she passed him without saying a word. Occasionally, she'd let go of a branch, knowing it was going to swing back and hit his face. Hearing him cry, "Hey!" made her chuckle. Greg used to do the same to her on their hikes through the woods. She had learned to keep alert.

Are you calm again, Amelia?

Winston's voice blasted through her thoughts as if someone were holding a megaphone to her ear. Amelia stopped and looked around.

Child, I asked if you are at peace. You were quite upset when I invited Meesha to come along on our journey. Inviting Meesha to accompany us was the only logical solution. Now I can watch him, you see.

Amelia cupped her hands around her mouth and shouted up to Winston. "Winston, are you talking to me?" He kept walking. Leaves drifted down through the cool air and fell silently to the ground. One landed on Winston's back and clung to his fur. "Winston?"

No need to shout. I am communicating with you telepathically, *as you say on Earth. We curlers call it mind-speaking. It is our gift. We can communicate with most anyone and, of course, hear thoughts. Well, experienced wizards can be challenging for us... Regardless, will you please keep up? Meesha will wonder why you have stopped, child.*

Mind-speaking? Wizards? She looked back at Meesha, who was still busy with his arrows and clearly wasn't hearing anything they were saying. Light shone on his jet-black hair, and she realized with a start that it was exactly the same color as hers, only as straight as one of his arrows.

Catch up, child! Meesha cannot hear me. He has had a sweep spell placed on him, and his mind is completely blocked. I cannot read his thoughts.

"Sweep spell?"

Hush, child!

She shook her head to clear it. Surely she was just imagining voices. Up ahead was a large, smooth-topped rock between two trees. *Maybe I can rest there for a bit.*

Winston cleared his throat. *Do not climb the rock, child. There is a little being sleeping under it that will surely sting you and perhaps kill you if you wake him. That would be most inconvenient for me. I don't know how I would explain your demise to Queen Fredonia.*

"Inconvenient for you?" Amelia shouted.

Winston swung around and glared at her.

"Why are you yelling?" asked Meesha.

"I... uh... never mind. I wasn't talking to you." Amelia placed her hand over her mouth. Winston nodded and continued on the path.

"Are all humans so rude?" Meesha asked.

"Only the ones that get arrows shot at their faces!"

Meesha kept quiet.

Amelia, it's important for us to communicate this way until I find out why Meesha has come to Gheir Island.

Winston, I hate this. Amelia pressed her fingertips to her temples. This was a total invasion. *Get out of my head!*

Relax, child. I know it takes some getting used to. You must understand, however, that if I am to protect you, our minds must be in sync. You have to keep your mind open. Do not try and shut me out.

So she could control this if she wanted to? She could try and stop Winston from listening in on her thoughts? Perfect. She didn't want to be someone's puppet.

I can understand what you're thinking child. Please...the harder you try to keep me out, the more I will persist, and we will both end up exhausted. You are not my puppet, I promise you.

Fine. Amelia wanted to open her mouth to speak. Her tongue moved with every word she thought. *Can you hear me?*

I can hear you.

So all this time, you've been listening to my thoughts? That's not cool, Winston.

Not cool? As opposed to warm? I don't understand.

Not cool means not good! You've got no right to my thoughts. It's an invasion of privacy. My thoughts are my own!

Waiting for them at the top of a hill, Winston leaned against a tree with his giant arms crossed and his lips pursed together. *I should stand by and let you hurt yourself with your terrible thoughts? I think not! Your mind is a very powerful tool, yet you humans have no idea how to use it. Thus it uses you.*

Who are you to tell me what I should think? What gives you the right to decide what's best for me? How dare he! *Calm down, he's listening now.* Amelia's foot slipped in the dirt. "Crap!" She caught herself before her face hit the ground.

Are you all right, child?

Yeah, I'm fine. So, if you've been listening to my thoughts all this time, then you know how much I want to find Greg. Why aren't you helping me?

Amelia felt Meesha standing right behind her.

Don't worry. Meesha can't hear you. Winston rubbed his back along the bark of the tree, pretending he wasn't paying any attention to Amelia or Meesha. *And I am helping you find Greg, child. Trust me.*

Amelia rolled her eyes. *I have to clear my mind. Puppies, kittens, candy...* She studied the forest; dirt, rocks, leaves, trees, yellow sky with blue swirls... cool air.... Amelia tried to control everything she thought. This was hard! Her mind was like a runaway stallion. She couldn't catch up to it, let alone control it.

"What are we waiting for?" Meesha whined.

"I'm resting, young man. I am not as young as I appear."

"Will we reach Keen before dark?"

"Most likely." Winston crouched down on all fours.

"Is it safe here?"

"I believe so."

"Perfect." Meesha ran past Amelia and plopped down next to Winston.

Amelia approached and cleared a space to sit. The *Book of Time* lay on the ground beside Winston. "Can I look at your book?"

"It's Queen Fredonia's book. Here." *This is not like books with which you are familiar, child. Take care.*

Amelia didn't respond, but ran her fingers over the tattered cover. Indigo letters spelled out the title of the volume: *Book of Time, Earth.* She brought the book to her nose. The faintly sweet smell was familiar, like gardenias, her favorite flower.

Suddenly, a scaly hand shot out from the pages and grabbed her wrist!

"No!" she shrieked.

The hand gripped tighter. Long prickly fingers squeezed her forearm. Still screaming, she jumped to her feet and tried to shake the book free.

"Winston! Help!" Amelia twirled around, hands flailing. "Get it off me!"

Meesha howled in laughter.

Relax, child! I told you this book was...unique. It is simply greeting you with a welcoming handshake. That is customary where you come from, is it not? "It will let go." Winston spoke calmly.

Amelia's chest heaved with every panting breath. "Okay," she took a deep breath. "Okay, let's see..." She reached out gingerly and flicked the book open with one finger. The hand instantly disappeared back into the book.

Meesha wiped the tears from his cheeks. "You looked ridiculous, human!"

Amelia glared at him. He smirked.

"Hush, now, boy. Amelia, sit down."

Being sure to keep the book open, she sat opposite Meesha and Winston. Her cheeks burned.

Winston pointed at the book. "Watch this, child."

Words at the bottom of each page rose into the air and floated in front of her. Above the words, images played out like a silent movie. One scene showed a busy farmers' market with villagers shopping from vendors, talking and smiling at one another. Beautiful orange flowers decorated the ground around them, and overhead, the sky was swirls of fuchsia, lime green and yellow.

"Whoa!" Amelia whispered.

"What has the *Book of Time* shown you? What does it say?" Meesha slid towards her, stretching his neck, trying to see over the book's cover.

"It's people shopping at a farmers' market." Amelia touched an apple cart with her finger. It immediately spilled, and the old apple seller began to pick up the apples and place them back in the cart. *How did I do that?*

"Most interesting... Keep watching, child." Winston crossed his long legs in front of him.

Meesha moved next to her. He leaned so close she could feel his hot breath. Being next to him felt oddly—familiar.

"Look!" Above the words and image, a tiny red light appeared. It began twisting and swirling spastically, like a severed electrical wire.

"Hey, that's what brought me and Greg here!"

"It's a String! Winston, come see!" Meesha was practically sitting on top of Amelia now.

"I was there, Meesha, I don't need to see it again."

"Where? I don't see you in the image." Meesha started to move the villagers around with his finger.

Amelia watched in amazement. "Try over there, Meesha." Meesha was rearranging the scene before them, but none of the villagers appeared bothered.

"Hey, there you are!" Amelia cried when she saw a small curler standing next to a beautiful woman in an emerald robe. "You're with Queen Fredonia! Look at you. You were adorable. How long ago was this?"

Many, many years ago, child...

All the townspeople were gazing at the bright light. Suddenly it struck the ground like lightning and then disappeared. Emerging from the exact spot where the light had hit were three bearded men carrying rifles.

"Winston!"

"Hush and watch."

The men were huddled together, rifles aimed at the crowd that was moving in closer to them.

Slam!

The *Book of Time* closed.

CHAPTER 15

"What just happened?!" Amelia tried to pry the book open again, but it wouldn't budge.

"That's all it's going to show you, child."

Meesha grabbed a low hanging tree branch to pull himself up. "Who were those men?" he asked.

Winston stretched and purred. He stood, shaking dirt from his fur.

"Please, Winston. Who were those men? Were they from Mystic or Earth?"

Amelia handed *The Book of Time* back to Winston.

Winston nodded. "We must go."

Meesha swung down from the branch.

Winston tucked the book under his arm. "I will tell you the whole story as we journey."

Amelia ran to Winston's side. Meesha sidled up beside her. She snatched an arrow from his quiver. "Just in case you get too close," she warned.

"Give it back!"

"Nope."

"Children, just listen now. Walk and listen!"

"Sorry, Winston," they demurred in unison.

"Back in 1769—your Earth time—three humans arrived in Mystic. No one knows how or why. They simply appeared in the midst of a bright red light. Creatures, nus, and wizards had never known of a place called Earth before that moment."

"Creatures, wizards, and what?"

"Nus," Meesha replied. "I'm a nu. Well, I could be a wizard, maybe... hopefully."

"So, Winston, nus are like people, only they can be wizards too?"

"Nus don't know if they're wizards until their powers appear," Meesha explained. "It could happen at any time. I'm almost thirteen, and I don't have any powers yet, but that doesn't mean anything. I could still be a wizard."

"You're what? No way."

Meesha frowned.

"It's just that you look younger...um...I'm almost thirteen, too."

"Amelia? Meesha? May I continue now?"

"Sorry... go on, Winston."

Meesha kicked the dirt as they walked and said, "I hate those men. The Three are the reason Mystic has changed. Mystic separated into two sides: the followers of Ralient and those who stayed loyal to Queen Fredonia. Before the humans came, Mystic was peaceful—they say it was a *utopia*. I've never known that life, and it's all because of the humans. They kidnapped Sri, and now Queen Fredonia has to hide, all thanks to them!"

No wonder Meesha shot the arrow at her. *Wait. Who's Sri?*

Winston nodded. "Sri was Queen Fredonia's only daughter, second in power to her mother and in training to take her mother's place as Guardian of Mystic. She was studying at Guin, a home for young wizards, when the Three arrived. Sri was the first to speak to the visitors, and she invited them to Guin.

"The Three—Daniel, Finley, and James they were called—lived at Guin for many months. They taught Sri and the other wizards about Earth, and they learned of our world. Time passed, and Sri's admiration for James grew along with her powers."

"And that's when everything fell apart," Meesha interjected.

"Shhh." Amelia bumped him with her shoulder.

"A wizard by the name of Ralient also lived at Guin," Winston continued. "Ralient had been best friends with Sri and was very much in love with her. Many of the wizards looked fondly upon Sri, as not only was she beautiful and kind hearted, but she was also incredibly talented in the use of her powers.

"Ralient wanted to marry Sri. He wanted to rule Mystic with her. But Sri did not return his feelings of romantic love. She thought of him only as a friend. Back then, if such feelings were not returned, it was accepted and believed that a new path must be followed—the correct path. However, Ralient grew more and more obsessed with Sri and refused to believe he couldn't win her over. Then he discovered Sri's love for James. He grew dark with rage. Love is a powerful force, and so is its opposite. Ralient's jealousy fueled his power, eventually making his power equal to Sri's."

"Mystic began to change. Where once everything was peaceful, there developed a haze of mistrust and ill will among Mystic's inhabitants. Fights erupted between neighbors. Some nus contracted sickness for the first time ever. Wizards concealed their powers instead of sharing their gift with others. Sadness and discontent spread like a plague."

"Ralient told everyone that the Three were to blame for all the terrible things that were happening in Mystic. But Queen Fredonia knew better. She came to our village in the Ice Hills and put a spell on all the curlers—the mind-speaking spell. Then she went to the Haans and pleaded for their help in protecting Mystic."

Meesha scoffed, "But Sri left!" He threw a rock into a thick bush. "She was supposed to stay and fix everything with the Queen, but she abandoned us for *your* world!" Meesha's hazel eyes shot daggers at Amelia.

"Don't get mad at me for something that happened in the past! I had nothing to do with it! Maybe those men never wanted to come to Mystic in the first place!" Amelia snapped the arrow and flung the two halves into the trees.

"Hey!" Meesha scrambled to pick up the broken arrow.

Winston, I know you can hear me. Will you please explain to Meesha that it's not my fault?

Meesha caught up to them.

"We are almost to the clearing. Just beyond the giant oak at the top of this hill is the field that leads to Keen. Come along." Winston used his tail to clear away some bushes blocking their path.

Winston? What the heck?

85

Did you not hear his anger, child? Telling him it's not your fault will be pointless. It will only add oxygen to his flame. He needs time to cool off before he opens to the truth.

Whatever.

Getting out of the forest would be refreshing. Change of scenery—that's what she needed. *Okay, Winston. Go on. I'm listening.*

"One night Ralient was out alone. Some say he had planned to kill the Three, and some say he was simply on his nightly stroll and had not yet become...well, what he is now. He encountered a Walterboro named Zef. Zef was a joyous Walterboro with a compassionate heart. He and Sri had been close friends. Perhaps that is why Ralient took his life. Dreadful to take the life energy of another being..."

Winston paused and gazed at Meesha who was back to sharpening his arrowheads. "Never before had there been a murder in Mystic. Ralient left Zef out on the boat dock for all to see and then hid Zef's blood-soaked jacket under James' bed. With first light, everyone gathered on the dock, horrified and fearful. The crowd blamed the Three, believing they brought chaos to Mystic. A mob, led by Ralient, made their way to Guin. Ralient led them to James' room. He held up the jacket and the crowd roared. James and the other two men were locked up.

"Ralient gave a speech in the market where the men had first arrived, trying to convince everyone that the humans must be killed in order to protect Mystic. He told them harmony would return once the humans were gone. Some wizards and nus retreated to their homes. Others gathered and discussed plans for getting rid of the foreigners.

"Sri used her magic to bring the men to this forest, hoping a String would appear. Ralient followed, and so did Queen Fredonia. And, indeed, the String did appear, whipping through the sky, making its way towards them. Just as the String touched the ground, Ralient lunged at James. Sri called James' dagger to her hand and sliced Ralient's face from his forehead to his chin. Ralient screamed in fury. He fell to the ground covered in a thick gray mist of darkness. Sri knew Ralient would never let James live, so she grabbed James' hand and stepped into the red light with Daniel and Finley. 'He needs my protection,' were Sri's last words. Her mother, the Queen, said, 'I will warn you if I sense you are in danger. Go!' Then she bade her daughter farewell. The red light glowed and the four disappeared.

"Ralient stood up and faced the Queen. He spat and smeared his blood across his forehead. 'It's not over,' he threatened. 'I will hunt them down, kill them both and rule Mystic.' Queen Fredonia offered him what he could not refuse—power in exchange for a promise from him to never go to Earth. Queen Fredonia presented him with an enchanted clay mask that would make him as powerful as she. But the mask had hidden powers.

"Ralient made the promise, snatched the mask, and placed it over his face. Immediately breaking his promise, he ran towards the glowing light. He bounced back and hit the ground. He could not enter. He tried to remove the mask from his face, but it held fast and would not permit him to transport beyond Mystic. He was trapped, and so Sri and James were safe.

"Queen Fredonia sent Ralient to the North West Vertices beyond the White Mountains, an area he named Gatineve. And since then, Ralient has been recruiting and capturing wizards and nus, forcing them to wear clay masks similar to his. Khalas are Ralient's warriors. Wherever Queen Fredonia goes, Ralient can sense her energy. His power continues to grow. She must always protect herself while looking after others, because if Ralient finds her, he could kill her and take over as Guardian of Mystic."

"What happened to Sri and James?" Amelia asked, mesmerized by the tale.

"Who cares?" Meesha cried. "Sri was selfish. She should have stayed with us instead of going back to protect those humans. She chose the Three over us." He threw down the stone he'd been using to sharpen an arrow and placed the arrow back in the quiver. "If it had been me, I would have let the men die."

"How can you say that?" Amelia retorted. "Sri did the right thing by protecting them. It was brave of her to leave. Think of all she gave up..."

"You say *brave*. I say *selfish*! What do you know of it, human? She should have stayed here, married Ralient, and ruled Mystic as was intended."

"Are you serious? You think the unrest in Mystic is Sri's fault?"

"Children!" Winston boomed. "Look!" The lion-man was standing tall, head raised. Amelia stepped out of the shaded forest and into a misty white light. Heat warmed her face. She breathed in fresh lavender. "What the—?"

◆

CHAPTER 16

They were standing on a lush carpet of bright green grass sprinkled with neon-colored wildflowers. Cobalt blue, fuchsia, electric orange—shocking. Their petals swayed in the breeze as if they were waving hello. And standing as tall as the Washington Monument in the middle of the field was an Egyptian-like obelisk.

Diamonds the size of her hand, grouped by color, formed a line down the center of each side of the Obelisk. Next to each diamond, a gold-plated name was etched into the stone.

"This is awesome! What is it?"

Meesha slid his palm across the smooth surface as he jogged around it. "I've never seen anything like this."

Winston pointed to the black diamonds on her robe. "Look familiar?"

"Cool, the diamonds match. Is that Mystic's symbol or something?"

"These are the names of revered wizards—Guardians who have ruled Mystic. As you can see, there have been many."

"So many..." Amelia shaded her eyes to try to see how far up the obelisk the names continued.

"This name you will recognize."

Amelia stepped closer.

Queen Fredonia

Suddenly the misty white fog that had stretched beyond the Obelisk lifted, and there, towering behind two wide banyan trees, was Keen.

It was not the castle Amelia expected. It was a massive dome with a circular mosaic door. A long staircase led up to the giant door.

"Come on!" Meesha shouted.

When they reached the landing, every bead on Amelia's Ayer was blinking. She spun the beads between her fingertips and felt their warmth. Amelia gazed at their distorted reflections in the mosaics as Winston tapped the door three times.

They waited. Nothing.

"Why isn't she answering?" Amelia knocked harder. The Ayer tightened around her wrist.

"I thought you said she knew you were coming," Meesha said.

"Patience, Meesha." Winston tapped again.

"Winston?" Amelia held up her glowing Ayer.

"You two wait here." Winston pushed the center of the door. His hand went right through the door with a loud whoosh. Winston chuckled. Then he disappeared inside as smoothly and quickly as a cat.

Meesha grabbed Amelia's arm. "Is he okay?"

Amelia stepped back.

"Come, children." Winston's voice beckoned them through the door.

Meesha stuttered. "Y-you go first."

She shook her head. "I think he's fine. C'mon."

Whoosh! She stood in front of Winston staring at the vastness of Keen. Bright light, cold air, and not a couch or chair anywhere.

"Well done, child." Winston nodded, then called to Meesha, "It's your turn...put your hand in the center and push."

"What is this place?" muttered Amelia when they were all together. She could hear the soothing sound of a waterfall, and turned in every direction searching for one, but couldn't find it.

They were outside somehow, but not entirely. Billowy clouds floated above their heads making it impossible to see a ceiling, the floor was crystal blue, and the walls were growing vines, twisting and weaving together as they climbed higher and higher. Tiny flowers decorated the vines. It appeared as though they were communicating with one another, the petals on the flowers opened and closed as if they were having silent conversations about their visitors. A cold wind blew through Amelia's dark curls and turned her breath into fog, but her robe kept her warm.

"It's freezing in here." Meesha rubbed his arms and legs, then his eyes widened. "Oh, look!"

A thick vine was descending from a cloud. Clinging to the side of the vine was a creature dressed in a purple satin robe with a ruffled white collar. His face was mint green. Purple freckles accenting his bubble cheeks and triangular eyes. It was his ears that were most impressive. They jutted straight out from the sides of his head, shaped more like giant turkey feathers than ears. His toes twitched as he spoke.

"Welcome, visitors! *Tee-hee.* I am Meeno. *Tee-hee.* Queen Fredonia has been waiting for you. *Tee-hee.*" Meeno's intermittent giggling was unnerving, but no more so than his leering at Amelia.

"What...who is that?" Amelia whispered to Winston.

Winston shrugged. "A wizard, perhaps?"

Meeno pointed a bony finger, and a spiral staircase made of glass appeared before them.

"Yes, indeed," Winston said under his breath. "Definitely a wizard."

"Follow the stairs. *Tee-hee.* Turn left down the long corridor. *Tee-hee.* If you make it that far, Queen Fredonia will find you." Two more giggles and *poof,* he was gone.

"W-what d-did he m-mean, if we m-make it that f-far?" Meesha's teeth chattered. His lips were turning pale blue.

"Come, we don't want to keep Queen Fredonia waiting."

A blue robe garnished with black diamonds was draped over the gold banister of the staircase. "Here, Meesha." Amelia tossed the robe to him. "This must be for you. And if it's not—well, you're freezing to death, so you may as well use it."

"Th-thank you!" He slipped off his quiver and covered himself. "Much better."

Winston was already on the third step, carrying *The Book of Time.* Amelia grasped the gold banister—it was smooth as ice—and took a few steps up, staying clear of Winston's tail. As they ascended, the vines on the walls seemed to be growing beside them. There was no ceiling or corridor in sight; only clouds, vines, and the endless staircase.

Cool mist drifted around them. Winston's tail swiped at the thickening fog, but it was still difficult to see. The robe clung to Amelia's body, keeping her warm, and she concentrated on the next step and the next. She was all too aware of a growing feeling within her—the same she'd felt in the forest. Unrest, like a dark cloud, loomed through her. *Winston, what's happening?*

But Winston either didn't hear or was ignoring her.

She glanced down through the clear glass steps. *Don't look down! Don't look down.* Amelia gripped the gold banister even tighter.

Winston began humming. Amelia's stomach clenched with each step. "Uh... could we..."

She thought she heard a whisper. She turned her head but no one was there. *Winston?*

"Trust."

Yes, she heard it more clearly now. Queen Fredonia!

"Did you hear that, Winston?"

"Hear what, child?"

"Queen Fredonia."

"What did she say?"

"Just—trust."

"Hmmm." Winston paused, then waved his giant hand to clear the mist from his face. He crinkled his nose, and his ears turned from side to side. "Climb on my back, both of you. Now!"

CHAPTER 17

Thunderous crackling echoed below them. Balancing on the trembling stairs, Winston scooped up Amelia and Meesha and positioned them on his broad back. In the process, *The Book of Time* fell, its pages rippling, sounding like hundreds of fluttering birds.

"Oh, no! The book…" Amelia reached for it.

"It's all right. Hang on, child."

Amelia buried her head in Winston's fur. He took off just in time. The glass stairs shattered beneath them. Winston flew higher and higher.

Finally, a sudden jolt and they landed on a corridor floating among the clouds. Amelia lifted her head and brushed her tangled hair from her face. Clouds… long pebbled path… sky. "It sure looks like a long way down."

Meesha groaned and slid to the floor. "Then don't get too close to the edge."

"Where are the walls? I thought corridors had walls." *Apparently not in Mystic. This makes me nervous.*

"Well, our Queen certainly knows how to entertain her guests," Winston mused as he smoothed down his fur.

"Entertain? I would've preferred some lime juice." Amelia rubbed her knees, willing them to stop shaking. "What happened?"

"The stairs are kaput."

"No kidding…" Amelia rolled her eyes at Winston. "But, why?"

Winston lifted Meesha to his feet. "Up you get, we've found the corridor and, unlike the staircase, we are all in one piece. Come along."

Two loud giggles emanated through the mist. Meeno appeared, cross-legged, toes twitching.

"Thought you should know you're being followed. *Tee-hee*. A Khala destroyed Her Majesty's beauteous staircase. *Tee-hee*." He wrinkled his nose and pointed his bony finger at Amelia. "It was carrying your human scent. *Tee-hee*."

"Being followed?" Winston bellowed. "Here?"

"Absolutely. The Khala hunts the girl for Ralient, of course. *Tee-hee*." Meeno shook his head. "I would hand her over and save your lives. She's just a human. *Tee-hee*." Meeno tilted his head. "Oops! The Khala has found you! Good luck! *Tee-hee*." *Poof*, he was gone.

"Run!" Winston commanded. And they ran.

"How did a Khala get in Keen?" Meesha yelled. "Did that creepy wizard let him in?"

"Where are we going, Winston? Shouldn't we fly?" Amelia panted. "Where's Queen Fredonia?"

A loud SNAP like two whips cracking together, reverberated above them, and a black shadow dropped from the sky. "Winston! Watch out!"

Winston stopped to encircle Amelia and Meesha in his giant arms. Amelia crouched as low to the ground as she could. The Khala's darkness seeped through to her bones.

And there it was, its eyes glowing yellow, unblinking, staring straight at Amelia, saliva dripping from its fangs. "Ahhhhhhhh!" the Khala screeched, sending shooting pain through her entire head.

"The...girl...mussst...come ...with....meee..."

"No!" Winston roared. "You leave her alone!"

The Khala screeched again, piercing their ears. Amelia knew what she had to do. She couldn't risk Winston's and Meesha's lives like this— the Khala wanted her, not them. She took a deep breath, ducked under Winston's arm, and ran. "No, child!" Winston hollered.

She kept running. And then she suddenly remembered—her mind flashed back to the woods on that horrible day. She'd been running then, just like now, the shrieking and the wings behind her, closer, closer...

"Go, Amelia! Faster!" Amelia blinked. Meesha was running right beside her. "Look!" He pointed ahead of them.

A shadow loomed.

"Run, Amelia, run!"

Wind from the wings blew across her neck. The Khala was close. Too close.

Meesha dove behind the shadowy figure.

"Queen Fredonia!" Amelia gasped.

The Queen raised her hand towards the Khala. Amelia dodged behind her, trying to steady her gasping breaths. "Don't let it take me. Please!"

Hovering just in front of them, the Khala gnashed its teeth and stretched its claws menacingly.

Queen Fredonia spoke, her voice echoing like some sort of god's. "You are not welcome in my home. You must leave at once."

"I ...will ...have...the ...girrrlll..."

"No, you will not!"

The Khala screeched and loomed at Amelia. "Leave her alone!" Meesha screamed.

The Khala hissed, flew in a tight circle, and came at them again.

Queen Fredonia raised her finger. A blinding silver light shot out, sending the Khala rolling backwards.

Amelia was dizzy. Without thinking, she stepped out from behind Queen Fredonia.

"Amelia, what are you doing? Get back!"

Meesha was yelling, but she couldn't make out his words.

Winston voice roared through her mind. *You are strong, he is weak. You are strong, he cannot control you. You are strong.*

"Winston?" She paused to gaze at the Khala, whose mouth seemed to be morphing into a masked face.

Queen Fredonia placed a firm hand on Amelia's shoulder. "Be brave. And trust...yourself."

Warmth filled her and Amelia's mind cleared.

"It's him," Amelia whispered. Ralient.

CHAPTER 18

"How much longer do you think you can protect her from me?" Ralient taunted the Queen. "You are losing your power, fair Queen. Gheir Island and Keen will soon be mine, along with your precious granddaughter."

"Amelia is home. Be gone from here!" Queen Fredonia shot her hands in the air, thrusting a ball of orange light at Ralient, who transformed into the Khala and took off, shrieking laughter thundering behind him.

Silence. It was over.

Granddaughter. Ralient said granddaughter.

Everyone was watching her. They were nuts. Amelia wasn't anyone's granddaughter. "I don't...I don't understand," she said cautiously. "What did Ralient mean?"

"Amelia, you have great gifts." Queen Fredonia's voice was gentle. "Gifts that will manifest as long as you are in Mystic. You're my beloved daughter Sri's child. You're my granddaughter. And you're a wizard, just like me."

"What...?" Amelia stumbled, sinking to the floor at the Queen's feet. A dull roar like the ocean, filled her head, and she tried desperately to catch her breath. She focused her eyes in front of her, noticing the black diamonds lining Queen Fredonia's robe. Exactly like the ones on Amelia's robe. Exactly like the ones on the Obelisk. And then she understood. The diamonds were not the symbol of Mystic. They were a family symbol. *Her* family?

Amelia shook her head. "You're wrong. This is all a mistake. I don't...I don't have any family." She was Amelia Ann Dean from Elizabethtown, Pennsylvania. She was *not* Queen Fredonia's granddaughter—and definitely not a wizard!

"Amelia, you were born after Sri and James left. *They* are your parents. And we believe you have been chosen by Mystic to take my place as Guardian."

Impossible. She was supposed to become Queen? This was getting crazier by the second!

We are not mistaken, child. Mystic has chosen you.

"No, no, no!" Amelia protested. "I'm not going to be *chosen* for anything. Look at me. I'm just a kid! A middle schooler who was crippled and who can walk again—not some wizard. You're all wrong!"

"Think back, Amelia...way back to when you were little. Were you ever visited in your dreams by any friends?"

Coral... but Coral was make-believe. Amelia remembered those nights alone in new foster homes. She'd close her eyes and Coral would appear. "Sing with me, Amelia," her imaginary friend would say. Coral kept her company.

Coral sounds a lot like Laural, don't you think? Winston's voice filled her mind.

"The voice!" Amelia whispered. *'It's me, Laural... please help me.'*

"Um... Amelia?" Meesha was staring at her feet.

"What?"

"Look down."

She was hovering and hadn't even noticed. "Ahhhh!" She panicked, flailed, and fell back to the ground.

"Um—that's not really how you fly," Meesha said with a laugh.

"*Fly?*"

Meesha pulled her up. "You're a wizard. And all wizards fly. Everyone knows that!"

"Mmm...well...I'm very happy with walking right now, thanks."

"You're crazier than I thought. Didn't you hear them? They told you that you have power. Maybe you're more powerful than Ralient! Did you ever think of that?

"Do you even know how to use that Ayer? Since you're a wizard, all those beads and combinations of beads contain spells. It's magic! Wizards use them for training until they can do the spells without them. They're special. Amelia, you better learn how to use that thing."

"My god, I just found out I was a wizard! Give me a break!" Amelia tried to remove her Ayer from her wrist, but it wouldn't budge. "Take it! I don't want it!"

"You can't just ignore us and let Ralient destroy Mystic. You have a duty to your land and your people!"

"A *duty*? My land! My people? Seriously? You just don't get it, Meesha. This is wacked."

Amelia turned from the three of them and began walking away.

"You always have choices, Amelia," Winston said calmly. "And no one can make you be something you don't want to be. But Meesha's right. You do have powers—and Ralient wants you for those powers."

Amelia had no idea where she was going. Queen Fredonia called after her, "Ralient is watching you, my child. He knows who you are even if you don't accept it. Be careful."

Amelia spun around. "How can I save Greg when I don't even know where I am or... *who* I am?"

"I can help you with that! *Tee-hee!*" Meeno appeared in front of Amelia. "Oh, great."

Meeno held out his three-fingered hand. A tattered scroll sat in his palm. "For you, Queen Amelia."

"Don't call me that. I'm not the queen...she is." Amelia nodded towards Queen Fredonia.

"Ahh, denial. It's the human in you. *Tee-hee.* Take this map, memorize it like *I know you can,* and leave it here. *Tee-hee.* Oh, and Queen..." Meeno hesitated. "I mean, Amelia, please learn to fly. *Tee-hee.* You will never survive another Khala attack on foot. They will tear you apart piece by piece, and then I would have quite a mess to clean up, yes...a nasty, nasty mess. *Tee-hee!*" He tossed the scroll to Amelia and disappeared.

Tear me to pieces? What's the matter with him?

"Open it, child." Winston, Queen Fredonia, and Meesha gathered around her.

"You open it." Amelia threw it to Winston. But the map turned in mid-air and flew back to Amelia.

"It will only open for you, my granddaughter." Amelia's eyes met Queen Fredonia's. And the Queen spoke to her mind, as Winston had done. *You remind me of her, you know. You have her will and her kind spirit.* "Well, child. Do you want to find Greg or don't you?"

CHAPTER 19

Amelia unrolled the map, and it transformed into an immense, levitating three-dimensional world. Mystic was not round like Earth, but a cube. Queen Fredonia turned Mystic like a Rubik's Cube, naming villages and mountain ranges.

"Here is Gheir Island, floating over the Nimi Sea. There is Draysia. Within Draysia is the city of Volarit..."

"Hey, slow down," Meesha interrupted. "Let me see Volarit!"

Queen Fredonia raised her eyebrows at the boy. "I...I'm..."Meesha stammered. "I'm sorry, I mean may I see Volarit please, Your Majesty?"

"Are you sure, Meesha?"

Meesha nodded."Please."

"As you wish."

Queen Fredonia touched the map and Volarit zoomed forward, bringing the village into full view. Thick black smoke covered the village and drifted over them.

"What the ..." Amelia breathed in soot and coughed.

"Hey!" Meesha swung his arms, trying to clear the air.

Queen Fredonia waved her hand, and the smoke disappeared. Piles of rubble littered the dirt streets of Volarit. Bodies were scattered on the ground. A patch of green grass beside an old shed was the only splash of color in the gray debris.

"No, no, no," Meesha moaned, grabbing the sides of his head.

Amelia whispered to Winston. "Ralient?"

"Khalas!"

Queen Fredonia stroked Meesha's shoulder. "I'm sorry, Meesha, there was nothing I could do. Ralient's power is getting stronger every day." She looked over at Amelia.

Amelia was quiet.

Winston pointed. "That's Ice Hills, where I am from."

"Winston, it's beautiful!" Amelia stepped forward. Rows of ice-blue glaciers stretched to the sky, bright light reflecting off their snowy peaks. A gust of cold air blew across their faces. "But where is everyone?"

"Ralient." Winston frowned. "It's only safe for curlers in Ice Hills to stay indoors now and communicate through mind speaking." He sighed. "Khalas don't like freezing temperatures, and Ralient can't break through the curlers thoughts. For now, they are safe, but they are fearful."

"Where's Gatineve? That's probably where Greg is... right?"

Winston nodded.

"Gatineve? Oh no, don't!" Meesha ran behind Winston.

Amelia waved her palm across the map.

"Almost there, child. Keep going."

"I... uh... Amelia, it's not a good idea..."

"It's just a map, Meesha! If we're going there to find Greg, we have to see what it's like."

Meesha peeked from behind Winston. "Who said I was going there?" He pulled his head back. "I never said I was going there... no way!"

"Be cautious. Ralient's darkness is great." Queen Fredonia inched closer to Amelia.

"Winston, Queen Fredonia, stop her! You know what will happen!"

There it is! Amelia moved her finger towards Gatineve. A bolt of orange light flew out from the map and hit Amelia.

"Ahhhh!" Amelia opened her eyes. She was lying on the floor. Queen Fredonia held her arm and the Ayer shone bright blue.

"Are you all right?" the Queen asked.

Amelia shrugged. "My arm is numb."

"You will be fine. Look at your Ayer, child. Each bead is a spell. Several beads can be combined together to form complex spells. All you must do is point your Ayer in the direction you want the spell to go, and it will sense your need. One day, when you are much older, you will no longer need your Ayer. The spells will be part of you."

Amelia saw the blue bead on her Ayer flash as she waved it over her arm.

"The blue bead on your Ayer is for healing."

"Yeah... I kind of see that now."

Meesha chortled. "Well, I'm sure not going to Gatineve."

Amelia sat up. "Fine."

"Now, now." Queen Fredonia pulled Amelia to her feet. "Ralient knows you will look for Greg. He will be waiting for you. Amelia, when dealing with wizards, you must understand that illusions can appear real." In a flash, the Queen morphed into the tortoise and then back to herself.

"Amelia, your best defense against Ralient is to listen from within. He can play tricks with your mind."

"Um...okay."

Meeno appeared again, looking very serious. "Queen Fredonia, Khalas are attacking the Haans! You must come quickly. I've summoned the Seer dragons. We're going to need their assistance this time."

"Of course, Meeno. I'm on my way!"

"I'll need the map," Meeno said to Amelia. She nodded, and instantly Meeno and the map were gone.

"Amelia, please wait here until I return," Queen Fredonia directed, concern in her voice. "You will be safer here than anywhere else. When I get back, we will figure out how to rescue Greg—together. Winston, I trust you will look after them?"

"Yes, my Queen. I wish you peace." Winston bowed. "Good-bye."

Queen Fredonia nodded "Good-bye, Winston... and Meesha."

"You're coming back, aren't you?" Amelia asked.

"Good-bye, Amelia, daughter of my daughter." Queen Fredonia raised her arms and disappeared.

"Why didn't she answer me, Winston? She told us to wait here for her, so she is coming back, isn't she?"

"Did you listen to anything she told you, child?"
"Of course I did."
"Well, then, you have your answer."

CHAPTER 20

"So, let me see you fly—Your Majesty." Meesha bowed deeply towards Amelia.

"What? Don't do that!"

"If you fly—and you can, you know—you'll be able to get us back down there. We won't be stuck up here."

"I think that's a brilliant idea," Winston said heartily. "All wizards must fly."

"I can't fly." Amelia rolled her eyes. "You can get us down, Winston."

"I would be robbing you of your gifts. It is time for you to learn, child."

"You can do it, Amelia—just try." Meesha peered over the edge of the corridor. "I can teach you. I've seen lots of wizards learn to fly."

"Lots?"

"Okay, one wizard. But I know I can teach you!"

"Um... okay." Amelia peered down. "Sheesh."

"Spring up into the air, and keep your body stiff and symmetrical. Like this!" Meesha jumped, his back ramrod straight.

"Yeah... and then what?"

"And then you just point your arms in the direction you want to go... easy!"

"If it's so easy, let's see you do it."

"Ha, ha. Very funny, Your Majesty."

"Stop calling me that! And anyway, maybe you're a wizard. Didn't you say you might be?" Amelia smirked. "You can find out."

Meesha shook his head.

"Come on, Meesha, let's show Amelia how it's done." Winston flew towards Meesha, grabbed him and sailed down off the corridor.

"Thanks, guys!" Amelia called. "Thanks for leaving me here all by myself!"

Well, at least she had her Ayer with its healing bead. She'd probably be able to heal herself—unless she died instantly from head injuries.

Amelia took a deep breath and closed her eyes. *I can do this.* Suddenly, she felt a hand on her back, and her body fell over the edge. Her stomach leaped to her throat. Panicked, Amelia turned her body upright, raised her arms out to the sides, then up over her head. It worked! She was standing in midair. *Don't look down.*

"You're welcome, little birdie. *Tee-hee!*"

That freaky little wizard had pushed her! But she was managing... somehow.

"Move your arms!" Meesha yelled from somewhere below her.

She lowered her arms to her sides. She didn't fall! Amelia swayed back and forth as if she were standing on a swing. *I'm flying!*

Amelia glanced down and pitched forward. Quickly, she raised her head and righted herself.

"Well done indeed, child, well done!" called Winston.

"Watch this!" Amelia twisted her arms above her head and twirled like a ballerina. "I want to see how fast I can go." Amelia stretched her arms out in front of her like Superman and let her body fall flat. She jetted like a bullet with air stinging her eyes and pushing her cheeks to her ears.

"I told you!" Meesha cried. "You're awesome, Your Majesty!" He laughed.

Amelia slowed and landed next to Winston and Meesha. "Thank you." Winston's face showed pride. "I can fly, Winston."

"Well done."

"So now what? I say we go and find Greg."

"We wait. That's what Queen Fredonia said to do." Winston flew the opposite direction from Keen's front door and stood in front of a wall of flowing water. He placed his hand in the spray—and vanished.

"Where'd he go?" Meesha ran to the water wall. "He's gone!"

Winston's face and dripping mane popped through the water. "Are you coming?"

Amelia didn't hesitate. She stuck her hand into the falling water and felt soft droplets tickle her arm. "C'mon, Meesha!"

Next thing she knew, she was standing in a cozy living room surrounded by bookshelves and a crackling fire from a well-tended fireplace. There wasn't a drop of water on her. "Cool." On a table at the far end of the room were baskets of rolls and bowls of sweet berries like the ones she'd eaten in the Walterboros' cave. Her stomach growled, and she bolted to the table. Winston held a glass of lime juice and pointed behind one of the bowls. Amelia spotted two more glasses of the wonderful drink, picked one up and popped a bubble in her mouth.

"To learning how to fly." Winston raised his glass.

"To learning how to fly, and finding Greg." Amelia clinked her glass to Winston's.

Meesha stepped through the wall. "Food!"

The three filled plates and made themselves comfortable. As she chewed contentedly on a mouthful of berries, Amelia spotted something peculiar about the books on the shelf. She almost choked. "Winston, those books are floating! And look! There's *The Book of Time.*"

"Mmmm, yes."

Amelia set down her food and approached the shelf. "If there're so many copies, why was it so important to go back to the forest to get that one you dropped?"

"Those are five unique books, child. Each one tells the story of its own world."

"Five? You're telling me there are five different worlds?"

The room suddenly lurched forward. Meesha yelped, and Amelia shot up into the air ready to strike.

"No need to worry. Gheir Island has just taken to the skies," Winston explained. "We are fine. Sit, rest and stop worrying, child. You're too young to worry so."

Amelia sat on a comfortable couch to finish her lime juice. Greg was out there somewhere, scared and alone, and she was filling her face. She was supposed to be this powerful wizard all of a sudden, and she still couldn't help her best friend.

Meesha and Winston began a conversation about sharpening arrow-heads. Amelia was full and not taking an interest in the conversation. Her eyes became heavy. Winston's deep tones lulled her to sleep.

"*Frére Jacques...Frére Jacques...dormez-vous...dormez-vous...*Amelia.... Amelia..." Amelia's eyes shot open. She was sitting in front of a great banyan tree on top of a giant hill, wind blowing her hair across her face. She brushed it away, trying to see who was singing that old nursery melody. "Cor...Laural? Is that you? Where are you? Laural?"

CHAPTER 21

"Yes, it's me, old friend! Amelia. Listen, you *must* find Jupiter. He will take you to Greg."

"Laural? Where are you? I don't understand!" Amelia tried to move, but the wind was holding her back. "Who's Jupiter? And how do I find him?"

"Find... Jupiter...Quai Mountains...Amelia... save us!"

Suddenly Amelia woke back on the couch. Winston and Meesha were standing over her. Amelia gasped.

Winston spoke softly. "What was your vision, Amelia?"

"We..." Amelia took a deep breath. "We have to go to the Quai Mountains. Someone named Jupiter's there, and he'll take us to Greg."

Meesha bounced with eagerness. "Come on then, Amelia...Let's go."

"Patience. Patience," admonished Winston. "Queen Fredonia said to wait here. And that's just what we shall do."

Meesha reached out to help Amelia up. "I'll go with you," he said rather grandly.

Amelia took his hand, stood up, then let go. She looked at Winston. "I can't...I'm not sitting around here and waiting anymore. Greg's in danger and I've wasted way too much time. Laural said to go to the Quai Mountains and find Jupiter... that's what I'm doing." Amelia flew to the water wall and turned towards Winston. "My best friend needs me. You come if you want to."

Meesha picked up his quiver, swung it over his shoulder, and followed.

It is dangerous out there, child. Winston's mind-speak reverberated in her head.

I don't care, Winston. Now's the time.

"You're going to have to carry me, Your Majesty, but I can get us to the Quai Mountains," Meesha said.

"Quit calling me that! Let's go." Amelia disappeared through the water wall. Meesha followed.

CHAPTER 22

The sky was deep burgundy with swirls of gold. Gheir Island was moving through Mystic.

Amelia scanned the sky for dark wings and yellow eyes. She knew the Khalas were out there somewhere, waiting for the perfect moment to attack.

Winston was carrying Meesha.

Fly low and swiftly. We are almost there. Winston's guidance comforted Amelia.

In the distance, an enormous and vast mountain peak peered over white clouds—the Quai Mountain range.

"How are we ever going to find this Jupiter guy?" Amelia muttered.

Look for a clearing, and we'll take cover for the night.

Amelia dashed down, scanning the mountainside. Gray boulders and trees far taller than poplars decorated its side. She spotted a flat field of grass with a winding stream snaking through its center. Along the stream's edge were colossal flowers and around them were…huge insects? Or were they birds?

"Oh, how lovely, look at all the Sneeds." Winston hovered next to Amelia.

Meesha brushed Winston's amber fur out of his face. "Wow, I've never seen so many before. Fly closer, Winston, let's see if one comes to us."

Amelia was mesmerized by the creatures moving swiftly from stem to stem, sticking out purple tongues to consume tiny beans from the center of each sunflower. Some raced like torpedoes while others lingered majestically like eagles. She wasn't sure she wanted to get any closer.

"Winston, what exactly is a Sneed, and do they bite?"

"Bite?" Meesha started laughing. "They're completely harmless. If you're lucky, one will choose you and be your friend for life." Meesha pointed. "Look, hold still—there's one coming towards us."

Amelia held her breath. The Sneed was flying directly at her face, its feathery wings swooshing the air. She squeezed her eyes shut and waited. "Tell me when it's gone," she muttered.

No one made a sound for what seemed an hour. She finally peeked and nearly screamed. Two giant eyes and a wide smiling mouth hovered in front of her. Wisps of cool air brushed Amelia's cheeks. She sent a thought to Winston. *Make it go away.*

You are being silly. He is harmless. Like a dog in your world, he simply wants to see who you are. Hold still.

Amelia stared into the giant blue eyes of the Sneed. His long brown lashes blinked.

"Maybe he wants to be your friend," suggested Meesha.

"I... uh... have enough friends..." *What am I saying?*

Meesha shook his head. "You're the weirdest wizard I've ever met."

Just then the Sneed's wings changed from feathers to two twirling rotors, and Amelia heard Meesha's voice replayed. "You're the weirdest wizard I've ever met." Then the creature took off like a bullet back towards the sunflowers.

Meesha laughed so hard he nearly fell from Winston's arms. "Sneeds record voices and play them back. That's how they communicate. Apparently he thinks you're weird, too."

"Ha Ha Ha!" Amelia mocked. "I've never heard of having an insect as a friend before."

Meesha laughed harder.

"Enough, light's fading," Winston said. "Let's camp with the Sneeds as this seems a safe spot." Winston set Meesha down.

Amelia landed on the bank of the stream. Sneeds flew all around her, but none came close.

She swished her hand through the cool water. "Nice." The sound of the stream flowing over pebbles and rocks was soothing, bringing her back to the summer days she'd spend in the woods with Greg. They'd throw their sneakers and socks off and wade into the freezing creek in search of crayfish.

Amelia stared at her reflection. She was really a wizard, but did she belong here with her grandmother? Grandmother. Was she ever going to get used to the idea?

A sudden chill crept up her spine. Silence. The flutter of Sneed wings was gone. "They're here," she announced. "Khalas!"

"Watch out!" roared Winston, just as one of the monsters swooped towards her.

Red, yellow, and green lights lit up on her Ayer, and Amelia thrust out her wrist, aiming the Ayer at the Khala's belly. A cube of green light shot from the Ayer and sunk into him, but as he tumbled backwards, two more Khalas swooped down, claws out, spitting and hissing terribly.

Amelia dashed into the air. She aimed the Ayer again, and another cube of green light shot out, but sailed just over the head of one of the monsters as it dove towards Winston and Meesha.

A Khala reached for her foot. She felt its claw pierce her ankle. "Ahhh!" The pain seared her like a fire! It yanked hard and then she was upside down in its grasp, blood dripping down her leg. "Winston!" she cried.

But Winston and Meesha were trapped by the Khala hovering directly above them.

Amelia launched her body upright and grabbed her captor's leathery talon. "Let go!" It squeezed tighter, then dove head first towards the ground.

The blue bead. Her finger found the bead and warmth filled her instantly, taking away the pain. *Thank you.*

Immediately she twisted the Ayer, aiming it at the Khala's fangs. A bolt of green shot out, missing its head but ripping a large rent through his wing instead. "Take that!" It clutched her ankle tighter as it fell. "Let me go!"

The ground rushed towards them at an alarming rate. Amelia fired another green bolt directly into the Khala's leg. Its grip loosened, and she was able to break free just before it crashed into the dirt below her with a sickening thump.

Amelia immediately arrowed off to help her friends.

"What are you doing? Escape while you can!" Winston yelled desperately as he fought to keep the Khala at bay. Winston was a blur of claws, his spiked tail flailing with great dexterity, but the sheer size and ferocity of the Khala was forcing him backwards while Meesha looked on helplessly.

"I'm not leaving you!" Amelia flew towards the fray but was afraid to use her Ayer with Winston so close to the Khala.

Winston tumbled to the side, narrowly avoiding the Khala's claw. Leaving Winston behind, the Khala pivoted and charged the now unprotected Meesha.

Amelia swooped in and tackled Meesha mid-air just before the Khala reached him. She hugged his body and rose through the air to escape.

"Thank you!" Meesha yelled as he craned his head back to see the Khala. "Amelia, hurry! It's coming for us!"

"Go, Amelia! Faster!" Winston roared. *I'm coming for Meesha.*

Amelia could hear the wings like cracking whips behind her. She couldn't fight holding onto Meesha. "Hang on!" Amelia shouted to him, spinning around and heading towards Winston.

"What are you doing? Are you crazy? It's gaining on us, Amelia!"

"Trust me," Amelia called back. "I know what I'm doing. Don't worry. Winston'll catch you." And she let him go.

"Heyyyyyyy!" Meesha squealed all the way down.

"Alley-oop!" Winston caught him and tossed Meesha on his back.

Wind stung her eyes as she descended faster and faster towards the mountainside. Her small size compared to the Khala's would have to be her advantage.

Winston's words were clear. *Perfect. Now turn west, follow the stream to a cluster of trees, there is a small cave—hide.*

Amelia landed and ran. The Khala was close behind. She ducked into the cave and covered her mouth, trying to muffle her heaving breaths.

Tree branches snapped and the sharp smell of charcoal burned her nose.

"You...will...come...out..." Saliva dripped from the Khala's mouth as he whispered outside the cave.

You are strong. You are brave. You are a wizard. Winston was with her!

Boldly, Amelia stepped out of the cave and noticed the gold chain and red pouch around the monster's neck. His eyes flared. "You...will...follow meee." The Khala lowered his face to Amelia's, snarling with hot, putrid breath.

Electricity bolted through Amelia's veins, and her Ayer shone brightly. "You...are...jussst...a helpless girrrlll..."

"I. Am. A. Wizard!" Three bolts of light fired from the Ayer, merged, glowed orange, and then engulfed the Khala in a bubble.

The monster screeched and hissed, beating its wings frantically and trying to break free.

She raised her arm and watched calmly as the bubble lifted into the air.

Amelia waved her arm to the side, the glowing bubble disappeared, and the Khala crashed to the ground. He stumbled, shook his head, and hissed angrily.

Amelia was ready.

But the Khala paused, then soared off.

She'd done it! Amelia threw her arms into the air and shouted, "Yay!"

Winston and Meesha landed in the clearing.

Well done, Amelia. Well done indeed.

"You're amazing!" Meesha cried. "I've never seen a wizard use the orb spell before. How did you do that without training?"

Amelia grinned. She had absolutely no idea how she'd done it. It had just come to her—kind of like breathing. Maybe it was because she would've died if she hadn't done what she'd done. "Lucky, I guess."

A sudden movement near her foot startled her. Instinctively she started to raise the Ayer, then dropped her hand when she saw what it was. The red pouch and gold chain. It must have fallen off the Khala's neck when he fell. "Look." She stooped down.

"Don't touch it; you don't know what it is," Meesha cautioned. He took out an arrow from his quiver and aimed it at the pouch, which flipped on its side. "I'll take care of it."

"No, don't shoot it!" Amelia cleared away the leaves around the pouch. *What do you think, Winston? Should I open it?*

That is a question for you, child. Is it safe to open? Does it seem safe?

Amelia took a moment. *Yes.* "I'm opening it. Meesha, don't you dare shoot me with one of those arrows."

Meesha frowned as she picked up the pouch. "Oh!" she cried, jumping a bit. There was something in the pouch. It bounced across her palm as she untwisted the thread that held it closed. "Hold still, I'm trying to set you free."

"Amelia, please be careful." Meesha backed up towards the bushes.

"Just one more sec..." The flap lifted and out popped a Sneed, flapping his wings and planting giant kisses on Amelia's cheeks.

"Ahhh..." Amelia wiped her face. "Stop! That tickles! Stop!" The creature's purple tongue was rough like sandpaper.

"It's a Sneed! And he loves you!" Meesha laughed.

"Enough...I get the message." Amelia started to back away, but the Sneed stayed right with her, blinking his gold eyes.

"He's very grateful to you for saving him," explained Winston.

Amelia wiped her entire face with sleeve of her robe.

Meesha patted Amelia's back. "I think you just made a friend, Amelia. He's yours forever."

And then they all heard Laural's voice coming from the Sneed: "Jupiter, get help, find Amelia."

"What did you just say?" Amelia offered her palm to the Sneed, who landed gracefully.

He spoke again. "Jupiter, get help, find Amelia."

"Winston, *this* is Jupiter, we've found Jupiter!"

"Yes, child. Though I think it's safe to say, Jupiter found us."

CHAPTER 23

"Hey, where are you going? Wait for us!" Amelia called after the creature, which flitted away from them. "Winston, come on, we have to follow him! He knows where Greg is!" Amelia took off after Jupiter, dodging branches and boulders to keep him in sight. *Greg, just hold on—I'm coming. I'm coming to save you!*

"Hurry!" Amelia gestured wildly to Winston and Meesha. "Down there!" She chased Jupiter down a steep incline and out onto the sand. She realized they were back on the shore of the Nimi Sea.

"Where's Jupiter?" Meesha called out to her. "I thought we were supposed to follow him."

Amelia jogged up the beach to Winston and Meesha. "Out there, over the water."

"And he's bringing company," Winston noted.

Three purple crosses sailed through the water following the tiny Sneed. "Haans!"

The three sprinted into the water to meet their friends. A giant wave crashed over them. Amelia laughed and swiped the water off her face. Meesha looked like a wet tomcat after a heavy rain, big eyed and bony. Winston guffawed and shook like a dog, sending droplets of spray everywhere.

Jupiter soared to Amelia's side, and the three Haans stepped onto the beach. "Wow! Ah...I didn't realize they were men." Amelia felt herself blushing at the sight of them. They were totally gorgeous.

"They're Haans. They have legs and feet on land and fins in the water. Rather more convenient than all this fur, I'd say."

"Um… Hi. I met you once… uh, before… remember?" *Nice. Way to make a good impression. Ugh!*

The youngest Haan spoke. "Queen Fredonia has sent us to tell you she and all the Haans are safe. She has been summoned to the White Mountains for a meeting with the Seer Dragons and wishes us to take you there to meet her."

"The White Mountains? Are you sure, lad?" Winston asked. "The White Mountains are not far from Gatineve."

"Winston, we have to listen to them, right? Queen Fredonia has sent us an order."

"Young man, since when are you in charge?" Winston studied Meesha, then turned to Amelia. "And what do you think, child?"

Amelia paused. Streaks of gold wove through the amber light. It wouldn't be a good idea to fly in the dark with Ralient's Khalas searching for them. If they were going to go, they should go right now.

Meesha's face was pale. A tiny bead of sweat was slid down his forehead.

"What's wrong with you, Meesha?" Amelia asked.

"What? Uh...nothing."

"Okay, then I think we should go with the Haans, Winston," Amelia said.

Winston paused and watched Meesha. "Then that's what we shall do." He motioned towards the Haans. "After you."

The Haans' long muscular legs disappeared and three fins popped up through the waves. Amelia watched the transformation. *This is going to be awesome!*

The youngest Haan waved to her. Amelia wiped her palms down her robe. *Stay calm. Relax.* She waded out to him and climbed on his sleek back, just in front of his fin. Meesha and Winston clambered onto the backs of the other Haans, and watched her from their new vantage points. *Sheesh, stop staring at me. I'm embarrassed enough.*

Jupiter hovered over her head, rotors spinning.

This was going to be some ride. Amelia caught herself taking deep breaths, readying herself to hold her breath as they submerged under the water. Habit.

They launched into the air. Amelia's body flew forward. Her stomach dropped to her feet.

"Yahooo!" Amelia squeezed her legs around the Haan's rubbery body. She threw her arms up. "Yahoo!" before they jetted down in a fast dive. *Splash!*

Water pressed tightly against her body, and she gripped the Haan as hard as she could.

"Don't be frightened, Amelia." The Haan turned his head, giving her a giant smile.

"Oh, I'm not scared. I think this is magical."

"I'm glad you like my home. This is the most majestic place in Mystic, in my humble opinion of course. I'm Blair, by the way."

"Nice to meet you, Blair." *Really, really nice to meet you.*

They traveled under water for some time before Amelia spotted Winston coming up beside her. Frost glistened on his fur. She hadn't noticed any change in temperature, so her robe must be protecting her from the cold.

"Are you okay, Winston?"

"My coat is quite thick. The Ice Hills are much colder than the White Mountains. This feels refreshing. Ahh, we are arriving already. There is the wall that leads to the White Mountains."

"Hey Amelia, how come your cheeks are so red?" Meesha had been waiting for them.

"Um...must be the freezing water, Meesha."

"I hope you have enjoyed your ride, my lady." Blair said.

"Thank you, kind sir... uh... I mean, Blair." *Really?*

"It has been an honor to assist you, Amelia. I hope we will meet again one day." Amelia's stomach did a little jig.

The two Haans that carried Winston and Meesha bowed their heads and then swiftly jetted away.

Huge mounds of ice jutting out from the ocean floor formed a wall in front of them. Colorful fish of all shapes and sizes swam all along the front and peeked from tiny indentations etched in the ice.

"Now what?" Meesha asked, trying to find an opening in the wall.

Winston pointed up. "We swim—up there."

"Come on." Amelia swam up the side of the wall, dodging to the left and the right as fish surrounded her.

"It's your fan club," Meesha called from behind.

Amelia nudged the fish gently out of her way to clear a path.

Winston reached out and pushed Amelia and Meesha to the water's surface. He popped up next to them with frost glimmering from his mane. Everything was brilliantly, blindingly white. Tall mountains, slender and pointed like newly sharpened pencils, lined the horizon. Amelia clambered up on top of the ice wall, letting the snow decorate her. The beauty of the mountains was stunning, but contrasted with the feeling that pervaded her being: Danger!

CHAPTER 24

Amelia searched the sky for Khalas. Nothing. Hopefully, Queen Fredonia would arrive soon.

Jupiter tickled her cheek with his fluttering wing. Amelia smiled. "There you are!"

"These robes are cool!" Meesha rubbed his sleeve. "I'm warm and dry. Not a drop of water anywhere."

Winston helped Meesha climb onto his back. "Let's go!"

Winston ascended, with Amelia close behind. They landed soon after on the snow-packed mountain. *Crunch!* The squeaky crunching of the snow underfoot immediately brought her back to her winters in E-town with Greg—before the accident, which she knew now had been no accident. Their snowball fights had been epic! Greg always won, but one time she'd come close to beating him. It had started out with laughing and snowballs lobbing through the air hitting more trees than bodies. But then Amelia pelted Greg in the head. It had been a mistake. She'd been aiming for his chest. Greg got mad, though, and had pelted her with one snowball after another. Neither one of them had given up, rolling around in the snow, tempers flaring. She was taller, but he was stronger, and he eventually pinned her to the ground, whooping and pounding his chest like Tarzan. "Okay, you win. Mercy!" she'd yelled, half laughing, half boiling, because she'd lost again.

"You can win all the snowball fights you want, as long as I get you back," she muttered. "Come on, Greg, where are you?"

Bam! A snowball thwacked her in the shoulder. A grinning Meesha looked very proud of himself.

"Oh, you're in trouble now!" Amelia rubbed her palms together then scooped up the snow and packed it tight. "You better run!"

Meesha took off. She chased him up a winding path, leaving Winston and Jupiter behind. Meesha was fast. She thought about flying to catch up, but figured that would be cheating.

"Come out, come out, wherever you are!" Amelia called, scooping up more snow into her bright red, tingling hands. "What's the matter? Is Meesha scared of a little snowball?"

Slow down, child. Where are you going?

I'm chasing Meesha. We're just having a little fun! Come join us!

Amelia tiptoed along the narrow path now, trying not to crunch too loudly. The path veered to the left. He had to be just beyond the bend. Slowly she crept, snowballs ready.

Meesha stood with his back to her, by a giant cherry blossom tree in full bloom, its light plum-colored flowers contrasting brilliantly against the snow. Beyond the tree were a ledge and the vast kaleidoscope sky. Wind whooshed through the tree's branches, swirling the snow in all directions.

Amelia dropped her snowballs and blew on her hands. "Meesha! What are you doing?"

But Meesha didn't move.

She took a few steps closer. For a moment, she thought the wind was playing tricks on her—whistling and humming like voices—but then she realized it was Meesha, who seemed to be whispering with someone. What was he doing?

"Who are you talking to, Meesha?"

Be still, Amelia. Winston was close behind her.

Amelia didn't answer, straining to hear Meesha and whomever he was talking with. She barely noticed her Ayer glowing and tightening around her wrist.

Amelia! Pay attention to your Ayer. It's giving you a warning.

All the beads on the Ayer glowed bright as stars. Amelia covered it with her hand and moved closer to the ledge. The voice. Could it be? Was

122

that... Greg? Yes! Meesha had found him! "Winston, come quickly! It's Greg!" she cried, bolting to the tree.

"Greg, we've been searching and...Oh!"

From behind the tree emerged a tall, masked man dressed in a long crimson robe with a high black collar. Long raven black hair cascaded along the side of his mask and draped over his shoulders, its highlights shining purple then blue as it caught the shifting light.

"Amelia, it is so nice to see you again. You look as lovely as this majestic tree."

Amelia started to tremble and turned to Meesha, who now stood beside her, looking down at the snow.

Amelia stay calm. Winston was next to her. His hair rose. He roared. "Ralient, back away!"

Do tell that humongous Neanderthal that you are calm and everything is fine. Now, now, don't look at me like that. Of course I can mind-speak. Ralient leaned closer to Amelia. Jupiter appeared over her shoulder.

"Here comes that silly little bug. I thought I did away with Jupiter when I captured Laural. I knew I should have killed him myself. It seems my Khalas have a weakness for Sneeds."

Ralient reached out to touch her. His arm met hers and sparks shot into the air, burning small holes in the leaves of the tree. Meesha scooted backwards and Jupiter disappeared into the tree's canopy.

"The young spy moves," Ralient said disdainfully. "What's the matter, Meesha, afraid you'll get burned?"

"Spy?" Amelia's eyes widened.

Meesha kept his head down.

"How does it feel to be betrayed by your own brother, Amelia?" Ralient hissed.

CHAPTER 25

"No! You're wrong!" Meesha yelled. "She's not my sister! She's human—and a wiz..." Meesha paused, looking frantically at Amelia.

"Come, come," Ralient scoffed. "You can't deny it. Born at the same time, triplets—two of three. To a rather wretched woman. Your foolish mother thought she'd separate you so I couldn't find you. I discovered Meesha living with that nu and her daughter in Volarit. Meesha led me right to you simply by being by your side...Amelia! It's only the third—your sister, Sara—who has eluded me. But not for long. After all, she is your sibling. I've found you two. Soon I'll find her. Your naive mother, Sri, always underestimated me."

Winston, what's he talking about? I have a brother and a sister?

Ralient cleared his throat. *Amelia, you are as daft as Sri. I can hear everything you're saying!* "Winston, will you please explain to this silly girl that I am the most powerful wizard in all of Mystic? She had better start believing it before she gets hurt."

Winston nodded. "Amelia, it's true. Meesha is your brother. You, Meesha and Sara are triplets. Sri was trying to hide you by keeping you apart. Together your energy would have been so strong, Ralient would have certainly found and killed you."

"Why didn't you tell me this back at Keen?"

"I didn't tell you in order to protect Meesha." Winston glared at Meesha. "Had I left him in the forest, or told him his true identity, Ralient would have killed him."

"And Sara? You could've told me about her! Wherever she is."

Winston said nothing.

Meesha started to sob. Tears streamed down his face. "Sri is *not* my mother. You *took* my mother and promised you'd return her and my real sister, Jia, if I followed Amelia. I've been with her since you dropped me in the forest. I brought her to you. Now set my family free."

Amelia faced Meesha. "Did you know Ralient would be here waiting for us? You planned to hand me over to him?" Amelia squeezed her hands into fists. She wanted to hit him. "You are not my brother!"

"I...um..."

"Silence, worm!" Ralient shot a continuous bolt of crimson energy into Meesha's body, pinning him to the ground in pain. "You did *not* bring Amelia to me. The Haans brought her."

"The Haans?" *Trust?*

"Stop!" Meesha screamed through the howling wind. "No more... stop!"

Winston ran to Meesha. "Ralient! Let him go. He's just a child!"

"You're pathetic, Curler." Ralient waved his hand and the light disappeared. He turned to Amelia.

Winston leaned Meesha's limp body up against the tree. Meesha sank into the snow. "You'll be okay, son."

Meesha was barely able to hold his head up.

"Did you really believe the great Queen," Ralient sneered, "would meet you in this nothing land of the Seer Dragons, so close to my home? I have discovered that most everyone will do anything to protect their family. It's simple: do as I say or they perish. Love is very powerful, especially when it's used for evil. Keep that in mind, little girl, and perhaps I will allow you to be of some use to me."

"I'll never join you—ever!"

"You *will* join me. Or I will kill Greg and make you watch. Who do you think you are, little girl?"

Ralient brushed his hand through the air and fired a yellow bolt at her. She ducked, but not in time. The bolt of energy slammed into her, knocking her backwards.

Winston flew to Amelia and cradled her.

Amelia's body convulsed. Her arms flopped to the floor then erupted with pain. "Winston, help!"

"The blue bead is here." He guided her finger over the smooth bead.

Thank you. The relief was immediate. Amelia twisted her Ayer around her wrist. The orange bead glowed brightly.

Ralient came towards them. Winston stepped in front of her with his arms out. Snow crunched under his colossal feet. "You may not take her."

Amelia heard Ralient's chuckle, and then a flash of red lit up the sky. Winston slumped to the ground.

"Winston!" Amelia cried as she rose and sent two orange cubes streaking towards Ralient. Then she reached down and held the blue bead over Winston. He sat up shaking his mane and spewing a flurry of ice crystals.

Ralient blocked the orange cubes and fired back. This time she raised her Ayer and deflected the bolts of light racing towards her face.

"You're learning. Good girl. But not quite good enough, I fear—"

Before he could finish speaking, Amelia pointed her Ayer, fired and sent him tumbling backwards.

"Fly away, Winston," she whispered. "Save yourself. Please!"

"Amelia," Winston said softly, "you must protect your brother."

"Who? Meesha? He's *not* my brother."

"He *is* your brother. You *must* save him. For your mother, for Mystic— save him." Winston stood up. He gazed into Amelia's eyes. *He is your brother, child.*

Amelia shook her head. "Go, Winston!"

Winston's words were clear in her mind. *Not without you, Amelia.*

Amelia saw Meesha clambering to his feet and sliding on the icy snow. She didn't notice Ralient coming towards her.

Amelia—Ralient!

"Defeating three Khalas and using the orb spell, Amelia? Mighty impressive. It seems you are...how should I say this... a mere seed just starting to sprout. One day your power will be great. You could prove quite useful to me in Gatineve."

Amelia crossed her arms but said nothing. "You see how this works is, I speak and then you speak. It's called communicating. Or hasn't your grandmother taught you such manners?"

Amelia glanced at Meesha then stared back at Ralient. *I hate you.*

"She's not coming with you!" Winston roared. Wind whooshed through his fur sending a spray of ice in all directions.

"Okay, you can refuse to speak to me, but I can still listen to your thoughts." Ralient ripped a branch from the cherry tree, leaving a line of red sap dripping like blood down the trunk. "Last I saw Queen Fredonia, your grandmother, she was lying on the sand in the Haans' village. Poor woman is getting old. She's not what she once was."

Ralient flicked the branch sideways. Out shot a red beam of light, which struck Winston in the knee.

"Ridiculous curler! I ought to kill you now and get it over with! Maybe that will make you talk, little girl."

Winston buckled over, grasping his leg and panting through his words. "Don't lose focus, Amelia. Ralient is just trying to distract you—and that's when you'll be at your weakest."

"Shhh." Amelia healed Winston's knee with her Ayer and helped him up.

"Now isn't that touching, Meesha? The fleabag curler has made a friend." Ralient circled Meesha, tapping his fingers together as he spoke. "Where were we? Oh yes. Amelia, you're coming with me, but before we leave we must give your brother his reward for being so devious. It takes a special person to betray his family. I admire that. What shall it be? A mask to cover his hideous face? Why, yes! I think that will do just fine. And, Amelia, so you won't feel left out, I've brought one for you as well. Winston, I'm sorry, but I find all that fur repulsive. I'm afraid you're not welcome in Gatineve. Quickly now, everyone say your good-byes before I do away with you!"

"Liar!" Meesha managed to yell. "You told me if I found Amelia and followed her, you would set my family free." Meesha wiped his eyes with the back of his hand. He paused and then pointed at Amelia. "Here she is." His voice broke, and tears ran down his face. He whispered. "I did what you asked. I want to see my real mother and Jia."

"Who's the liar here, Meesha?" Rage at Meesha's betrayal coursed through Amelia. "All this time you were lying to me and to Winston?"

"I had no choice!" Meesha whined. "You would have done the same!"

"Oh no, I wouldn't. I wouldn't betray my family like that. How could you?" Amelia flew to Meesha and jabbed her finger in his chest.

"Go on, girl—kill him!" Ralient clearly relished every moment. "What's the matter? You think it isn't in you to kill? Well, what if I told you little Meesha here helped me capture your darling Greg?"

"Whaaat?" Amelia reeled around to face Ralient. "What are you talking about? Where's Greg? What've you done with him, you monster?"

Ralient snickered.

Amelia swung back around at Meesha. He held an arrow in front of him. "Oh, you think that's gonna stop me?"

Calm, Amelia. Calm. Ralient's energy is filling you. Let your light surround his darkness. You are stronger than he is. Winston's thoughts rumbled through her mind, but she was too fraught to think.

"You were with Greg? And you didn't tell me?" Amelia grabbed the arrow and threw it down inches from Meesha's foot.

"Thatta girl! Now kill him!" Ralient swirled his arm, and a gust of icy wind blew Meesha to the ground.

Meesha scrambled to stand, but Amelia placed her foot on his leg and glared down at him. Her hair whipped around, and freezing snow fell on her face. "Answer me!" Amelia shouted, raising her arm with her Ayer. "Answer me!"

Meesha tried to free his leg, but Amelia pushed down harder.

Meesha begged, "Please, Amelia. I didn't mean to hurt you or Greg. I just wanted to save my family."

Look at his face, Amelia. He's frightened. Causing someone to fear you is weakness not strength.

Ralient's evil thoughts entered her mind blotting out Winston's. *He has humiliated you. Your own brother has betrayed you.*

There was panic in Meesha's eyes. She had seen that look and those eyes before. Eyes that resembled her own. Her mind flashed to a scene from when she was little. A woman with long black hair huddled the three of them close. Sara was crying. The woman's breath smelled of peppermint, and she whispered her words, "This is not good-bye forever. This is good-bye for now. Each of you is a piece of me, and that means that no matter where you are, we are always together. Remember… always." Then the woman was gone.

Another scene followed in Amelia's memory. Amelia was at a park. She was on a swing, with a kid on either side of her. A smiling woman with long black hair was standing in front of them. "Hey Meesha, watch me. Pump your legs like this, and you'll go higher."

"Meesha?" Amelia tried to remember more but the scene faded.

"Say good-bye to the curler!" Ralient shot a bolt of light.

Amelia screamed, "Nooo!"

Winston tumbled backwards and skidded through the snow inches from the ledge.

"Winston, hold on!" Amelia ran towards him, yelling.

Winston's body was convulsing. Between groans, he called to Amelia, "You are stronger than Ralient."

"Not true, Neanderthal!" Ralient flew up in the air and spun around. A black bolt of light jetted from Ralient's hand and hit Winston, sending him careening off the ledge, and slamming Amelia into the tree.

Winston's roar echoed as he fell.

"Winston!" she cried. Just then, Jupiter dropped onto her shoulder from a branch. Amelia whispered, "Go help him."

Jupiter took off, buzzing right past Ralient.

"I hate that Sneed! He's as good as dead." Ralient peered over the ledge. "Poor curler. That bug's not going to save him." He shook his head. "Now, where were we? Oh yes. Amelia, kill Meesha!"

Meesha cried, "I remember, Amelia. The woman with long hair...she told us we were a part of her, and wherever we were we would always be connected."

Amelia flew to Meesha. She crossed her arms and stared.

"That's my girl. Now, get rid of him."

Amelia raised her Ayer. Meesha cowered.

Winston's voice boomed through her mind. *He's your brother!*

Winston?

Curler! She's mine!

Amelia swung around and shot a bolt of light at Ralient.

It hit Ralient in the chest, knocking him to the ground and sending him skidding along the ice.

Amelia grabbed Meesha's arm. "I believe you're my brother, but what you did—"

Meesha interrupted. "Amelia...I'm so sorry! I had no choice. I found Greg trapped in a cave in Volarit. He told me a Khala had taken him and he needed to get back to you. I showed him a secret passage to escape, and hid him in a shed near my house. It was only hours before Khalas came searching for Greg and destroyed our village. I went to find my baby sister, but a Khala grabbed me and made me take him to Greg, threatening to kill my family. What was I supposed to do, Amelia? My mother, my sister...he was going to kill them."

"You could have been honest! If you'd just told me..." Amelia let go of his arm. "Fine. I'm still mad at you, but I want you to help me find Greg."

Meesha stepped forward, reaching out. Amelia backed away. "I will. Don't worry, Amelia, we'll find him."

"Oh, how disgustingly sweet. Now I'm going to have to kill you both." Amelia jumped in front of Meesha and faced Ralient.

Suddenly, a swirl of yellow light twisted over their heads. Amelia dodged and tried to deflect it with her Ayer, but she was too late. It draped over Meesha's body, knocking him unconscious.

"No!" Amelia kneeled at Meesha's side. She waved the glowing blue bead over his body. He didn't move. "Meesha? Please wake up." Amelia cradled his head in her arms. "Meesha."

Suddenly, Amelia felt herself being raised into the air. She flailed her arms and legs. It was no use. Everything was a snowy blur. The wind howled, but Ralient's eerie tones cut through.

"You are weak, little girl. Come with me, and I will take care of you. Together we will be the Guardians of Mystic."

Breathe, Amelia. Don't resist. Allow him in, and know you are stronger.

Winston! Amelia gasped for air. Every part of her being was trying to keep Ralient from taking control of her mind. *Let him in?* Images of Ralient's attacks on villages played like movies in her mind, as if she were right there witnessing the killing, deaths, and darkness. He was sucking the life right out of her, making her like him—evil.

You are strong. Let go! Believe in yourself. Winston persisted.

The ground trembled, the kaleidoscope sky twirled. Queen Fredonia appeared, hovering over the Cherry Blossom tree, Jupiter and Winston by her side. "Let her go!" Queen Fredonia pointed, and Amelia was released.

Amelia lowered herself onto the snow in front of Meesha.

Amelia held the glowing blue bead of her Ayer over Meesha. "Get up, Meesha. You can do it. Get up."

Queen Fredonia shot a bolt of green light straight at Ralient. With a rasping chuckle, he shot back, and the two lights collided, sending sparks like fireworks flickering through the air.

Meesha took Amelia's hand. She helped him to the tree and said, "Stay down."

Ralient fired a red cube of light at Amelia.

"Look out!" Winston roared.

Amelia raised her wrist with the Ayer and shot a cube of green light. The two spells collided and exploded.

Ralient bellowed, "Ahh, here they come. Ready for battle—for blood. My precious Khalas!"

A dark cloud of Khalas was approaching. The sound of wings whipping through the air sent chills through Amelia.

Just as she was about to call to Winston, everything went dark. *Help!*

When light returned, she was airborne with Meesha, Winston and Jupiter, floating beyond the ledge. They were trapped in an orb spell—enclosed in a bubble: unable to move, unable to speak. White noise filled her ears. Her eyes begged to close.

Captured. Where was her grandmother?

Then darkness.

CHAPTER 26

Amelia squinted in bright light. The air smelled of sweet honeysuckle. Jupiter fluttered in circles above her head. She rubbed her eyes, realized she was lying on the ground, and saw feet surrounding her.

A circle of masked nus stared at her. *Oh no—Gatineve!* She glanced around—Winston and Meesha lay on the ground nearby. As the three of them struggled to get up, the crowd stepped back.

"My sweet darlin', where *have* you been?"

The beloved voice was all too familiar, but Amelia wasn't going to let Ralient trick her again. She stiffened, readying herself for an attack. She raised her arm, aiming her Ayer—then hesitated.

A baseball cap covering white curls...librarian glasses...*Because I Can* T-shirt...Grandma K.!

"Is it really, really you?" Amelia whispered.

"Well, darlin', who else would it be? You look a little peckish."

"But we thought...we thought you were..." Amelia ran into Grandma K.'s open arms.

"My, my, my, I see I've been missed. It's okay, darlin'. It's okay." Grandma squeezed her tight and rubbed her back.

"You're alive!" Amelia mumbled into Grandma K.'s shoulder. "You're alive!"

"Hush, darlin'." Grandma K. stroked Amelia's hair. "Why are you so upset, darlin'? And where's my Gregory? Did he go off and find a football game somewhere?"

Amelia pulled away, wiping her tear-streaked face. How could she tell her the truth? How could she say, *Greg's gone?*

"Wait a minute! *Look* at you! What is the matter with me? You're standin' on your own two feet! I always knew you would walk again. You've got that spunk. Always have."

Amelia rubbed her palm along her forehead.

"Why that lost look, darlin'? It can't be all that bad."

But it was. It *was* all that bad. Amelia glanced at Winston. He nodded.

"Greg's...gone. I mean...uh... he's missing. He was taken." She broke down right there in front of everyone. Some wizard she was, sobbing uncontrollably, hoping somehow that Grandma K. could fix everything.

Grandma put her hands on Amelia's shoulders. "Don't you worry, sweetie. We'll find him. Trust me. I know my Gregory is just fine. He's feisty like his Grandma. We'll sit down with some sweet tea and figure all this out. You calm yourself down now."

"Grandma K., Greg thinks you're dead. *I* thought you were dead."

"That surely is the most ridiculous thing I ever heard."

"We saw you, though—we saw you lying on the ground after that car crash!"

"Car crash? What car crash? I've been here the whole time. The strangest thing happened, darlin'. I woke up the mornin' of our campin' trip and this woman appeared out of nowhere right there in my bedroom. I thought maybe she was an angel, and I was a goner. She told me her name was Queen Fredonia and said you and Gregory were in danger. She said I had to come with her to help you. Well, I just started to laugh. I began to think my mind was getting the best of me. Goin' crazy, you know?" Grandma K. tapped her head.

"It was horrible, Grandma K. It was raining, the car went spinning, we hit a tree, and then you wouldn't wake up."

"No, no, I was fine. Queen Fredonia just waved her hands, a map appeared, and woo-wee it was somethin'. She showed me this beautiful place called Mystic. I couldn't believe my eyes or ears, but what was I goin' to do, darlin'? She was either magic or I was dreamin', but whatever it was,

I figured I didn't have a choice. So I agreed to come with her. Next thing I knew, I was here! She told me to wait for you. She was goin' campin' in my place, and she would lead you to me. And here we are! But...where are we exactly, I wonder?"

"That's it! That's the drawing I saw in the Walterboro's cave! Queen Fredonia talking to Grandma K.! Winston, I told you it was a clue." Amelia clapped her hands. "Greg's going to be so excited to see you, Grandma K. I can't wait to see his face." Amelia hugged Grandma's arm and rested her head on her shoulder. "So it was Queen Fredonia driving the Ford Falcon all that time!"

Winston took Amelia's hand. "I know where we are. The Queen rescued us with her orb spell and sent us to Orra—a hidden land. Laural was the first to escape from Gatineve. That was some time ago. Laural knew there were others who wanted to escape, so she built Orra with the Queen's help. They created a secret passage connecting Orra to Gatineve. Ralient has not yet found Orra." Winston waved his arm across the crowd. "It is because of Laural that these fine folk are free from Gatineve, but not free from the mask."

"Darlin', who are your friends?" Grandma K. asked.

"This is Winston, my guide. He's helping me find Greg. And Jupiter. Jupiter is Laural's friend and, well, Laural's missing, too. And that's...um... Meesha. My brother—"

"Your brother? Darlin', what are ya talkin' about?"

"It's complicated, Grandma K. I'm still getting used to it myself."

Meesha stepped forward. "It's nice to meet you." Meesha bowed.

"Hmm. Hello there, young man." Grandma K. studied Meesha.

Jupiter flew around Grandma K.'s head and then stopped and blinked. Grandma K. laughed. "Oh my. You're a lil' rascal."

Winston brushed through his mane with his paw. "I am pleased to make your acquaintance."

"So formal, big one? I'm Grandma K."

Winston bowed. "You may call me Winston."

"Well, I have no idea what y'all been talkin' about—Laural, Gatineve, and Ralient. Are they friends of yours? I say let's get us some grub and, Amelia, you can catch me up on the happenings, all right?"

"Okay y'all...time to go home." Grandma K. shooed her hand at the crowd.

"Grub? Excuse me, ma'am, what is *grub?*" Winston asked.

"I'm no ma'am, big one."

"Food, Winston," Amelia explained. "Grandma K. wants us to eat."

"Great!" Meesha patted his stomach. "I'm starving. Let's go."

Grandma K. was already power-walking down a cobblestone path.

"Oh, yes, that does sound splendid. I could use a glass of lime juice."

Grandma K. spun around. "You mean that bubbly rainbow drink everyone's been tryin' to get me to taste around here? That ain't food. I'm cookin' us a *real* meal. A Pennsylvania Dutch meal."

"Of course, ma'am, as you wish."

"I told you. I'm no ma'am."

"Excuse me... I meant to say Grandma K. My apologies."

"Where'd you find this one, Amelia? The eighteenth century?"

Amelia chuckled. "Nope, I found him on the beach."

"What is Pennsylvania Dutch cuisine?"

Amelia did her best Grandma K. imitation. "Shoo fly pie!" Then she shot into the air and flew ahead of Grandma K. "Did I mention I'm a wizard and can fly?"

"Mel! My goodness now, you be careful up there! This is all too much. I'm an old lady, ya know. Don't go scarin' my heart to death. Come down here! A wizard?"

"Yeah, I can do spells with this." Amelia held up her wrist with the Ayer. "Mystic is pretty awesome, Grandma K. Well, except for the Khalas and um...Ralient." Amelia landed next to Grandma K. and skipped beside her.

Everywhere Amelia looked, she saw brilliant color. Bright blue and orange domed houses with white roofs, and flowers pushing up through green lawns. Palm trees and banyans were scattered throughout a park filled with nus playing and enjoying the beautiful day. Some even waded in a giant fountain that decorated the center of the park. And it was strange how the temperatures changed from one place to another. Just a short time ago she was freezing in the White Mountains. Now she was in paradise. *I could live here.*

They strolled up to a large house that looked very familiar.

"Home again, home again, now let's do a jig." Grandma K. chuckled at Winston's curious face. "Excuse me?"

"Welcome to my home, big one." Grandma K. held the front door open for them.

"It's your kitchen!" Amelia said. The kitchen was *exactly* the same as Grandma's on Poplar Lane! Photos of Amelia and Gregory decorated the refrigerator, one showing Greg approaching a basket dribbling a ball and Amelia with her arms up high, feet planted on the driveway in front of the net. She had her eyes shut tight and her face in a grimace. She remembered that day well. She'd had a bruise on her butt for weeks after that. Totally worth stopping Greg from getting a two-pointer.

"The fridge, pictures, all my stuff from back home, they were just here, darlin'. I don't know how any of this got here. Heck, I don't know how *I* got here. But I'm here, so might as well make the best of it." Grandma started to pour iced tea into flowered plastic tumblers as she spoke.

"Grandma, is this your famous sweet tea? Meesha, you *have* to try this, it's the best!" Amelia handed a glass to Meesha.

He gulped it down. "Awesome!"

"Here you go." She handed Winston a glass of tea.

Winston took a sip and wrinkled his nose.

"Not what you expected, big one?" Grandma K. patted Winston, her small hand disappearing deep into his fur.

Winston cleared his throat. "It's Winston."

"Okay, first we'll snack on some pie, and then I'll get to the real cookin' while you all discuss how we're goin' to find my Gregory."

Grandma led them into the dining room. "It can get lonely around here. So I keep myself busy by bakin' shoo fly pies. Help yourselves!" She gestured towards three pies decorating the dining table.

Winston sat down, placed his napkin on his lap, and examined the pies intently. "Nowhere in *The book* does it say anything about humans eating flies. I find the thought rather disturbing."

Jupiter buzzed around Winston's head, then towards the pies, then back at Winston.

"He's worried that if humans eat insects, maybe he'll be eaten too!"

Amelia laughed. "You're safe, Jupiter. Don't worry, we wouldn't eat you."

Amelia squinted at Winston. "His feathery wings would tickle our throats." Amelia winked at Grandma K. "Shoo fly pie is a delicacy."

"Yes, can you believe that Queen Fredonia even had a box of the dead critters waitin' for me?" Grandma K. tried to keep a straight face.

"I suspect you are teasing me. A fib you call it...right?" Winston said dead-pan to Grandma K., who sat down at the head of the table.

Grandma grinned. "Now, would I do that?"

Winston finally smiled. "Yes, I believe you would!"

"Ya' got me, Winston. I'm just teasin'. Now go ahead. Cut a giant piece for yourself and enjoy." Grandma raised her eyebrows. "Be careful, though. Sometimes the wings get stuck in your teeth. You may want one of those toothpicks when you're done." Grandma pointed to a clear container of toothpicks in the center of the table.

Winston took a giant bite. "This is simply delightful. Flies or no flies."

If Amelia didn't know any better, she'd say the two were flirting with each other. Weird.

"Oh dear me, the light has gone dim. I guess a storm's comin'. Look outside."

Meesha jumped up and pointed at the window. "That's not a storm! That's a shadow!"

Jupiter was playing Laural's voice. "Run away, escape!"

Amelia shouted, "Khalas!"

CHAPTER 27

"**H**urry, Amelia!" Meesha yelled.

"Glory be! What on Earth?" Grandma's fork clinked on her plate. "What's goin' on?"

"C'mon, Grandma!" Amelia grabbed Grandma's hand and led her through the house to the back door.

"What's happenin'? Where are we goin'?"

"Grandma, you *have* to be quiet," Amelia whispered. "They'll hear us."

Amelia dragged Grandma K. behind a fat bush. Meesha and Winston joined them.

Grandma pointed above their heads. "Mercy! Look at that!" Wisps of black swirled through the magenta sky. Khalas were everywhere!

"Follow Jupiter!" Winston's deep voice bellowed.

Jupiter was flying towards the tall fountain in the park. Familiar screeches filled the air.

"Run faster, they're coming!" Meesha cried, grabbing an arrow from his quiver.

"Meesha, take Grandma K. Follow Winston and Jupiter."

Grandma hesitated. "But what about you, darlin'?"

"Just go... I'll be okay. Really! Just go—you'll be safer!"

Meesha took Grandma's hand. "C'mon."

Villagers scattered through the streets, screaming and searching for cover.

Six Khalas swarmed down from the clouds, a black tornado headed right for her. She dodged behind banyans, leading the Khalas away from the others.

The Khalas landed, hissing, "Ahhh... meeel...yaaa."

Winston shot up into the air, Meesha under one arm and Grandma K. under the other.

Be careful, Winston!

Grandma K. hollered, "Grandmas don't fly! Put me down!"

Hovering by the fountain, Jupiter called to Winston and Amelia, playing Meesha's voice over and over. "This way! This way!"

Winston's mind spoke to Amelia. *The only escape is through the fountain spray and down into the tunnel. Jupiter has shown us the secret passage from Gatineve to Orra. The Khalas are too big to fit through. We'll hide in there until Queen Fredonia can rescue us.*

Winston, keep them safe. I'll catch up.

The fountain belched water high into the air. Jupiter waited until the water reached its peak, then dove down and disappeared.

"Ahhh... meeel...yaaa." Each Khala hissed her name.

Amelia ducked behind a banyan, held up her wrist, and shot a ray of turquoise light, which projected her image onto a park bench to distract the Khalas. A group of them took to the air and swarmed the bench, clawing at it, ripping it to shreds. Winston dodged past them, gripping Meesha and Grandma K. and plunged down into the spray, disappearing into the water. The Khalas tried to dive down too, but the water spit them back out into the air with a loud whoosh.

A Khala's wings snapped the air right over Amelia's head. She aimed her Ayer and shot a green ray at its wing. Gray smoke snaked out, but the Khala kept coming.

All Amelia saw was a sea of black with glowing yellow eyes coming towards her. She reached for her Ayer, but it was too late. A Khala snatched her around the middle, its razor-sharp claws trapping her arms to her sides.

His moist, putrid breath made her gag. She closed her eyes, shielding them from its spewing saliva. "Ahhhh!" Amelia twisted, trying to set her arm free, but the talons just dug deeper. "Help!" Amelia kicked her feet, but it was no use. The Khala was too strong.

It was taking her higher and higher, several hundred feet above the fountain. Saliva blew across her face. She dropped her head and gasped. Blood poured down the Khala's talon. Her blood. "Help me, Grandmother."

Light flashed, and Amelia felt herself suddenly falling. She threw out her arms to steady herself, but she was dizzy, losing consciousness, her eyes were shutting...

The blurry twisted body of the Khala plummeted beside her.

Amelia, wake up! You must *heal yourself. Now!* Queen Fredonia's voice focused her mind. Amelia tried to position the Ayer over her stomach. She pushed her arm against the wind, but the pain was too great. *I can't.*

You must. Amelia, you can. Now!

Amelia forced her eyes open, saw the verdant land rising to meet her, and wailed with all she could muster, swinging her arm across her body and tumbling head over feet. Blue light surrounded her, immediately taking away the burning in her gut. Her mind cleared. She threw her arms out to her sides and froze upside down, inches from the ground. *Sheesh!* Amelia flipped and landed on her wobbly feet.

There, in front of the fountain, was her grandmother. Amelia flew to Queen Fredonia's side. "Thank you."

"Don't thank me. You saved yourself. Know that."

Clouds of black headed down towards them. "Go Amelia! You have to protect the others. You are ready to face Ralient and save Greg. I will stay and fight the Khalas now."

"I can't leave you."

"You must. My time is ending, and yours is just beginning." Queen Fredonia reached for Amelia's hands. "Hold still." Her grandmother's power surged through her, strength and joy and hope all braided together. It was pure light.

"*Now,* Amelia!"

Letting go of her grandmother's hands, Amelia sprang up into the air. The Khalas screeched behind her, but she didn't look back.

The fountain spit water into the air. Flashes of light like fireworks exploded behind her.

Familiar words uttered by Queen Fredonia rang out through the Khalas' screeching. For the first time, Amelia understood their meaning. "Sei debole, sono forte!" *You are weak and I am strong.*

The water was at its peak. Amelia took one last look at her grandmother. Would she ever see her again?

Amelia, trust.

I'll be waiting for you.

Go!

Amelia dove into the water, down into the tunnel, into the darkness.

CHAPTER 28

The sharp stench of sulfur made her stomach churn. She wiped the sweat off her neck.

Flickering candles lining the walls cast eerie shadows around her, but at least it wasn't pitch black.

Shuffling in the darkness, trying to catch her breath, Amelia thought she heard something. "Winston?"

"Ahhh....meeel......yaaa!"

"Winston?" Nothing. She tried to call to Winston's mind. *Where are you? I'm in the tunnel.* "Ahhh...meeel....yaaa!"

Amelia backed up against the wall and counted her breaths.

There was a shadow in front of her. *Is that you, Winston?*

The shadow moved towards her. It wasn't big enough to be Winston. She stood frozen, tense, ready to strike.

"Hey, clueless!"

Electric blue eyes stared at her.

"Oh my god, Greg!" She ran and hugged him. Her Ayer glowed green, indigo, and yellow brighter than she'd ever seen. She squeezed him hard and then stepped back.

"I'm so sorry. I'm so sorry!" The words tumbled out of her. "I'm so sorry for being mad at you, and I'm so sorry I got us into this mess. It's a long story, but Greg—"

"It's okay, Amelia. *I'm* okay. Don't worry about it. It's good to see you. Where've you been?" Greg crossed his arms, and his eyes seemed to dart away from her.

"What? I've...I've been looking for *you*." Amelia paused." Are you really okay, Greg?"

"Yes, of course I am. Why wouldn't I be?"

His voice was so flat. Lifeless. *What's wrong with him?*

"So, uh...Greg, it's really great to see you. Have you seen Winston yet? I've been looking for him."

"No."

Amelia grabbed Greg's arm. "Greg, Grandma K.—she's alive! Can you believe it? She's really alive! I've seen her. Isn't that great? She's with Winston."

"Grandma's here? That's wonderful, Amelia."

Wonderful? Since when does Greg say wonderful*?*

"Are you sure everything's okay, Greg?"

"Yeah, sure." Greg rubbed his hands together. "I'm fine. Why?"

"I just thought you'd be more excited to hear about Grandma K., that's all."

"I'm excited." He took Amelia's wrist, sending a small shock up her arm. "C'mon. We've got to go."

Greg's fingers were covering the Ayer now, but little slits of light still shone through.

"Greg, how did...how did you escape from the Khalas?"

"Long story. I'll explain later." He picked up the pace, practically dragging her along.

"Where are we going?" Sweat was dripping down Amelia's face. "Are you sure this the right way?"

"Yes, this is definitely the way."

"Wait a sec! Did you hear that?" Amelia strained to glance behind them, but Greg tightened his grip, pulling her faster. "Maybe it was Winston?"

"No. I didn't hear anything."

"Um... maybe we should go back—"

"We have to find them, Amelia. Just keep walking."

Up ahead, the walls of the cave appeared to be moving—closing in. "What's happening?" She squinted, but everything was getting blurry. "Greg, wait. I think I have to rest. I don't feel good. Wait…"

"Amelia, you're not making any sense. Hurry!"

"Doyouknowahwherahh…" Amelia's tongue was like lead, her words slurring together. "Gre…."

"Keep going. We're almost there."

Sleep, that's all she wanted. Sleep. As she stumbled, an image flashed into her mind.

A tall dark-haired man in a tan robe stood in a field, staring coldly at a couple in the distance. They were holding hands, embracing, and then kissing. The woman had beautiful long black hair. The man had curly brown hair that covered his ears. And then Amelia knew who they were. Sri and James. Her parents.

She wanted to run to them, to call out to them. But she was unable to move or make a sound. The sky morphed from bright yellow to gray. As the man in the field continued to watch the couple, he became surrounded in a dark mist. Somehow, Amelia could feel this man's pain. Rejection, jealousy and anger were consuming him, leaving not a speck of light or hope. He wanted to *kill* them. As he wiped his hand across his face, his turquoise eyes ice-cold, his robe turned a deep crimson. Ralient.

Amelia's eyes blinked open. She and Greg had reached the end of the tunnel. He dragged her through some sort of canvas tent, and they stumbled onto sand—they were in a sweltering hot desert.

"You!" Amelia muttered through numb lips.

Horrid laughter filled her ears. She yanked her hand from Ralient's painful grip.

CHAPTER 29

"Foolish girl!" Ralient hissed. "The only way to capture you was to lure you to Gatineve. Your weakness, my dear, is caring far too much for your friends. It distracts you from listening to your instincts. Don't worry; the longer you are with me, the easier it will be for you to overcome that weakness. Lesson number one—trust no one. Everyone is your enemy. Once you are able to watch your friends suffer, I'll know you're ready."

Amelia reached for her Ayer but fumbled. *Where is it?* Heat radiated from the sand under her feet and burned her face.

Ralient flicked his wrist. A black ray hit her and sent her skidding sideways through the sand. "Do *not* challenge me, little girl. Your magic is no match for mine."

Amelia rubbed her eyes and spat out a mouthful of sand. A huge fifty-foot stone wall surrounded Gatineve. Khalas, perched like gargoyles, stood guard the whole way around. A massive brick building spewed smoke. Masked villagers peeked at Amelia from openings in the tents that made up the walled city. When Ralient turned his head in their direction, they disappeared inside. The only sound was the whistling wind blowing funnels of sand in every direction. *This is hell.*

Before she could get to her feet, Ralient scooped her up. Excruciating pain, like knives ripping into her skin, shot down her legs. "Ahhhhhhh!!"

Amelia writhed around, but couldn't break free. "Please... stop!" She screamed.

"You don't remember, do you? That day in the forest, running from my Khalas? You were supposed to die, but your dear devoted mother showed up and saved you." Ralient kept a firm grip on her wrist, his hand covering her Ayer, and tossed Amelia over his shoulder. "Paralyzed instead of dead, you were lucky. And now Mystic has healed you. Well, let's see what I can do about that." Ralient paraded her around the village and shouted at the sky. "You see, Sri? Your children are miserable and weak!"

Amelia tried to pull the arm with her Ayer free. Sweat dripped down her forehead into her eyes. "Make it stop!" *Let go of me!* She screamed as the feeling drained from her legs. Somehow that was worse than the pain.

"You tried to hide your precious triplets from me by separating them, but you failed. I found two of the three, and they're mine!"

He carried Amelia around Gatineve, shouting, "I have the girl! Mystic is ours!" The Khalas screeched and hissed wildly.

Amelia kept trying to reach her Ayer. Ralient's energy was draining her. If she could just hold her Ayer over her legs, she'd be able to heal herself and fly away.

Ralient dropped her to the ground. "Did you forget, silly girl? I can read your mind. I guess there's only one way to make sure this Ayer never heals you. Cut it off!" A machete appeared in his hand. He pulled Amelia's arm straight and raised the machete.

"Don't touch my daughter!"

Ralient released Amelia's hand. Amelia sat up. There in front of them, long black hair flowing around her beautiful face, and dressed in a lavender robe edged with black diamonds, was her mother—Sri.

Sri's soft voice washed over her, bringing back a flood of lost memories to Amelia: curling up on her mother's lap, listening to stories about fairies and magical lands, or coloring pictures of horses while her mother baked cookies.

"What color, mommy?"

"It's your creation, Amelia. Use your imagination, sweetie."

Her mother... she remembered.

"Let Amelia, Meesha and their friends go, and I will stay."

"I see where your daughter gets her weakness. It's been a long time, Sri."

Sri kept silent. Amelia waved her wrist over her legs, the blue glow soothing and cooling the pain instantly.

Ralient spun around. He spoke, his voice deep, his eyes glaring into Amelia's. "Make one move and I will kill you both."

Sri reached toward her daughter, "Amelia, my child."

Ralient now glared at Sri. "You think you can just return and I will forgive you? You are a foolish woman."

"I know you better than that, Ralient. I am not here for forgiveness. I am here to bargain—my life for the lives of my children and the three others you have captured. After all, it is me whom you really want."

"No!" Amelia cried.

"Amelia, hush!"

"Oh, I don't know, Sri. Only killing you when I could take *all* of your lives? That sounds so… anticlimactic."

The Khalas bellowed and hissed.

"Amelia is growing in power, Ralient. You and I both know that one day she will be far stronger than you. Let my children live, and she will stay by your side and rule Mystic."

"No! I won't! How can you—"

It is the only way, Amelia. Sri spoke to her mind. *Greg and Grandma K. will return home, Winston too. You and Meesha will be together to look after one another. If Ralient gives his word and we bind it, you will all be safe.*

Amelia's Ayer glowed red. "I'm not letting you do this!" She raised her wrist.

Ralient turned and fired a bolt of electricity that hit the sand right next to her. Amelia covered her eyes. "Don't you move, little girl!"

No Mother! Kill him! He's disgusting! You can't leave me here!

Ralient burst out laughing. "Does no one listen to me when I say I can *hear* you? Speak out loud, ladies. So much to learn. I can see training Amelia to obey me will be a challenge. One I greatly look forward to."

All the beads on Amelia's Ayer lit up. The lights swirled in front of her: orange, blue, red, indigo, green, yellow. She waved her wrist in the air.

"Amelia, don't!" Sri leaped to her side, grabbing her arm. She pulled Amelia close, tears filling her eyes.

"You left me," Amelia whispered.

"I love you, Amelia. Trust me."

"Uh...excuse me, but I believe we were in the middle of a negotiation, were we not? You're wasting my very valuable time. So what about Queen Fredonia? What would *she* say about your bargain?" Ralient sneered. "Have you received your dear mother's permission to make such a deal?"

"My mother cannot be found."

"She helped me escape," Amelia said. "And then she was fighting Khalas!" She whirled out of Sri's embrace to face Ralient. "What have you done with her?"

All the Khalas rose up into the air, beating their wings. Ralient laughed and held out a piece of shredded emerald green fabric with a single black diamond. "Such a pity. Poor, poor grandma."

"I hate you!" Amelia spat.

Ralient pretended to wipe tears from his eyes. "Already my little protégé is making me proud."

Sri put her arm tightly around Amelia and said, "Ralient, do we have a deal?"

Ralient nodded.

CHAPTER 30

"**I** won't let you do it!" Amelia hugged her mother and sobbed.

"Shut up! Quit your bawling or I'll feed you to the Khalas for dinner."

Sri pulled Amelia closer.

"So many wont's daughter. Life blossoms with wills." Sri kissed Amelia's forehead and wiped the tears from her face. "The wonderful thing about love is that it cannot be held in your hand or be seen standing in front of you. Love is magic. It's like air. Breathe it in, and it fills you. My love is with you, daughter—always." Sri let go of Amelia and faced Ralient. "You will allow me to say good-bye to my son."

"Of course," he sighed. "But make it quick. I am losing patience." Ralient pushed past Sri and Amelia and waved for them to follow. Nus came out from hiding in their tents, held their open palms toward Sri and bowed as they walked by.

"I feed and house them, and it's *you* they bow to?" Ralient scoffed. "They will suffer for such disrespect."

The three entered the brick building. It was lit by flickering torches. Statues of Ralient lined the walls. An iron fire pit, with white flames snaking to the ceiling, sat in the center of the room.

Ralient waved his hand, and the fire disappeared. The sound of clinking of metal came from above.

"I believe you know these people well, little girl." Ralient laughed.

Slowly, a hanging cage lowered from a chain in the ceiling. It rattled and creaked all the way down. Inside were shadows clinging to the bars. Amelia recognized Winston's silhouette. Sri took Amelia's hand.

Amelia gasped. "Let them go!" She wanted to fly up to her friends and set them free. Sri shook her head.

Winston! Can you hear me? Are you okay?

"Yes, Amelia. We are all fine. Shh. He's listening.

Grandma K. called out, "Amelia darlin', I was so worried about ya!"

"It's all right, Grandma."

Meesha was on one side of Grandma and... there was one more.

"Greg!"

Ralient squeezed Amelia's neck. "You will speak when I say you can speak."

Amelia's body crumbled under his grip. She tried to fling her wrist around and attack with her Ayer, but he forced her to the ground.

"Let her go! You're hurting her!" Greg screamed.

"Please, Ralient. That is enough!" Sri spoke firmly and placed her hand on Ralient's. He stared at Sri with an empty gaze. "Take your hand off me," he said coldly.

"Amelia will learn to obey me, starting now!" Ralient pointed at Greg. "And you, boy, shut your mouth, or your precious friend will suffer far worse."

Through half-shut eyes, Amelia noticed Grandma K. whisper to Greg. He nodded and folded his arms.

"You see, Amelia," Ralient said, "fear is what controls everything. Are you paying attention?" Ralient pinched her neck once more and then shoved her from him.

She looked at Greg. "I'm okay."

The cage rattled loudly as it met the ground.

"Ladies and gentlemen, your lives are being spared." Ralient dragged Sri and pushed her up against the cage. "Her life for yours."

"M...mama?" Meesha reached through the bars.

"Yes, Meesha, darling, it's me. It's me."

"No!" Meesha shook the bars of the cage. "Don't kill her!"

"You are an awful, awful man!" Grandma K. hugged Meesha.

"Old woman, you are as bad as these obnoxious boys with their horrendous outbursts. Such brave imbeciles while they are trapped behind bars." Ralient clapped. "I applaud your dramatics." He paused, "However, I demand respect! Let's get on with it!"

Ralient snapped his fingers, and two Khalas appeared. "Take the long-haired boy out."

Winston leaned close to Meesha, whispered something in his ear, and nudged him towards the cage door. A Khala opened the door, and Meesha stepped out. The cage slammed shut behind him.

"You have two minutes to say your good-byes."

"Wh...what?" Meesha's voice broke.

Sri huddled with Meesha and Amelia. "You two *must* take care of one another. Promise?"

Meesha shook his head. "You can't..."

"Meesha! Hush, now. Trust me." She paused and gazed at Meesha. "Good-bye, my loves. Trust."

As Sri hugged them tightly, Amelia felt something jump into her hand. She clasped her fist around it quickly. Feathery wings fluttered against her fingers. *Jupiter!*

"Time's up!" Ralient bellowed.

A Khala wrenched Sri backwards.

"Mama!" Bawling now, Meesha kept his arms wrapped around her waist.

"Meesha...please..." Sri begged.

Amelia had her hand gently clutched around Jupiter. "Meesha..."

Ralient waved at the Khala holding Sri. "Take her outdoors, and call the other Khalas to their feast. When you bring what's left of her back to me, I will set the others free."

Sri reached towards Ralient. "That is your word, Ralient? If so—bind it with the spell."

Ralient turned his back on Sri. "Take her away!" he commanded.

A Khala shoved Meesha away with its clawed foot. He groaned in pain as two Khalas wrestled Sri to the ground, tying her hands behind her back and her feet one over the other.

"Bound like an animal for slaughter!" Ralient scoffed. He spat into his palm, and a vial appeared. Ralient handed it to the Khala. "You'll need this to kill her."

They carried her away.

CHAPTER 31

Meesha took off after Sri.

"Meesha!" Amelia screamed.

Ralient threw his arms into the air. "Oh, just kill him too." The Khalas chased after Meesha.

"Ralient!" Amelia perched Jupiter on her collar and fired a green cube at Ralient, knocking him to the floor. Ralient shot back, hitting Amelia with a purple beam that lifted her and sent her hurtling backwards across the room. *I am strong, he is weak.* She was able to stop herself in midair just before hitting the cage.

Greg cheered. "Go get him, Mel!"

That's right, Amelia. You are strong, he is weak. Winston's support rang in her head.

"Oh, Amelia darlin', you are somethin'!"

Ralient flew towards her. "Silly child, give up now, and stop wasting my time." He flung his hands forward, and a bolt of lightning came sizzling at her.

Amelia crossed her hands in front of her face and watched it fizzle away. Immediately, she shot back and hit Ralient in the leg. He toppled over.

"Yes!" Greg yelled.

Black mist poured from his wound. Ralient cupped the mist in his hand, formed it into a tiny ball and blew it away. "Bravo, little girl." Ralient stood, brushed himself off, squared his shoulders, and calmly opened the cage door. "Get in, or I shall kill them one by one."

Amelia paused.

"Now!" Ralient reached in to grab Greg, lowering him to his knees. "He will go first."

"I'm coming!"

Ralient sneered. "Your loyalty is disgusting."

Amelia was almost through the cage door. *Loyalty. The wolf on Greg's Ayer!*

"Jupiter, attack!" Amelia reached towards Greg.

Jupiter darted back and forth and spun furiously around Ralient's head. While Ralient was distracted, swiping at the Sneed, Amelia pulled Greg out of the cage, held up his wrist with his Ayer and hers and aimed them at Ralient.

Winston put his massive arms around Grandma K. "Cover your eyes!"

Light gleamed white, and sparks hit the cage bars. Suddenly, out of Greg's Ayer leapt a huge wolf with teeth bared, pinning Ralient to the floor.

Ralient writhed under the wolf and shot a spell that sent it tumbling into the shadows.

Amelia waved her Ayer, and a yellow cube of light hit Ralient, sending him careening across the floor. He applauded. "Nice try!" He immediately fired back at Amelia.

Greg and Amelia ducked. The bolt of electricity hit the cage. Winston rolled backwards, his tail slamming into the cage bars. Grandma K. fell onto her stomach. Half her body hung out the cage door.

"Help me!"

"Grandma K.!" Greg yelled.

Winston flew to Grandma K., scooped her up and dashed out of the cage. Jupiter buzzed beside them.

Ralient came towards Amelia. *I am strong. He is weak.* Her hand trembled. She raised her wrist. Her entire Ayer glowed burgundy, the color of dried blood.

Suddenly Ralient flung his hand around and pointed at Greg. From out of the shadows, the wolf leaped onto Ralient, knocking his arm sideways just as he cast a spell. A black ray hit one of Ralient's statues, which exploded.

Ralient was trapped beneath the snarling wolf, its jaws tight around his throat just under the mask. Amelia stepped over to him and held her Ayer ready.

"Well done, Amelia," Winston said as he joined her, with Greg, Grandma K. and Jupiter.

Sri burst into the room with a limp Meesha in her arms. "Look! See what evil your Khala has done to my boy!"

Ralient started to laugh, but the wolf dug his fangs deeper into Ralient's neck. "Nasty beast!" Ralient sputtered.

"Heal him! You gave the Khala a potion—he used it on Meesha instead of me!"

"Revenge."

"Heal him!"

"No."

Meesha began gasping for air.

Amelia crouched down beside Ralient and whispered so no one could hear. "Save him and I'll leave Mystic."

"Get this beast off me!"

Amelia motioned to Greg. Greg nodded. "Off." The wolf obeyed. Ralient stood up, and the group surrounded him in a loose circle. Amelia kept her hand on her Ayer.

"Quickly, Ralient. He's dying."

Ralient glared at Amelia.

She nodded.

Ralient waved his palm, and a vial of pink liquid appeared in front of Sri. "Go on—take it."

Winston snatched it. "Wait!" He held the vial to his nose. "It's poison!" Winston threw it against the wall. A pink mist dispersed across the floor and disappeared.

Sri screamed at Ralient as she handed Meesha to Grandma K., "There's no redemption for you. You're horrid!"

Ralient's laughter rang through the room.

Amelia's Ayer glowed indigo. Without words, Amelia and her mother moved in unison and fired spells at Ralient. The spells collided and formed a black diamond that hurled towards him.

Ralient intercepted the diamond with a continuous bolt of silver light. A shock wave echoed throughout the chamber as the opposing spells collided. "Nice try, ladies!"

For a moment the spells seemed evenly matched, but slowly the diamond pushed closer and closer to Ralient's chest. He inched backwards. His arms began to quiver.

Amelia whispered, "Sei debole, sono forte," as the diamond crashed into Ralient's mask, shattering it into pieces.

Ralient covered his face and slumped to the floor. After a moment, he lowered his hands and raised his chin, his turquoise eyes glowering with rage. "That was a mistake! Go ahead. Kill me. Meesha will die too."

"Heal him!" Amelia had her Ayer aimed at Ralient. Sri was at her side.

Ralient smiled. He sat up and ran his fingertips down the sides of his face. "The real me."

The wolf growled, baring his teeth. Jupiter fluttered next to him.

Ralient closed his fist and opened it. A vial appeared with pink liquid. "In exchange for my life."

Winston reached for it, and Ralient pulled back. "You don't trust me?"

"Hurry! He's not breathin'!" Grandma K. shook Meesha.

Winston roared. "Give it to me!"

Ralient relinquished the vial. Winston's whiskers twitched as he brought it to his nose. He nodded at Amelia and Sri, and then took Meesha into his arms and poured the liquid down Meesha's throat.

"You and your Khala will leave Mystic and never return." Sri held out her palm. "Bind it."

Ralient stood and reached towards her. Sri hesitated then placed her palm on his. Their hands gleamed silver and green. Sri pulled her arm back as Ralient began to slowly disappear.

His deep chuckles echoed off the walls. "Poor, poor, Queen Fredonia, trapped and very much alive—so far from home. She's a world away from Mystic."

He continued to fade until only his sardonic grin was visible. "Perhaps I will join her." He vanished.

CHAPTER 32

Greg's wolf howled.

Greg patted his head, "He's gone!"

Amelia turned to Sri. "What did he mean? Where's Queen Fredonia?"

Meesha stirred and opened his eyes. Sri ran to him and stroked his head. "She's alive...somewhere—in another world."

"Earth? Could she be on Earth?" It was as if Greg had read Amelia's thoughts.

Sri nodded. "Maybe."

"Then we'll have to find her," Amelia said, joining Sri. Winston gave Amelia a knowing glance.

Sri placed her hand on Amelia's shoulder. "Of course, daughter."

"Well, Queen Fredonia's alive, and that's what's important," Grandma K. said. "And Meesha here is lookin' himself again."

Winston set Meesha on his feet and held him steady. Meesha gripped Winston. "What happened?"

"Ralient's gone and you're well." Sri hugged him. "Thank you, Winston for looking after my children. You too, Grandma K."

Winston bowed.

"I love that gal of yers. She knows it, too!" Amelia ran to Grandma K. and hugged her.

159

. The wolf sat calmly now at Greg's feet. Greg gazed down at him and gently patted his head.

Meesha picked up some pieces of the shattered mask. It turned to dust in his hand. "Is he really gone?"

"Gone from Mystic? Yes," Winston replied.

Sri led the group outside. A crowd of villagers filled the streets, cheering. Masks lay scattered on the sand.

Amelia watched the celebration before her. "Look at them!"

Meesha pushed his way through the crowd. "Mom! Jia! You're here!" A little strawberry blonde girl jumped into Meesha's arms.

"Amelia, it's Jia and my mom...um...my other mom." Before Amelia could say a word, Meesha was swept up in his mom's arms. Tears cascaded down her face.

"C'mon Greg, there's still something we have to do." Amelia searched the crowd. "Jupiter! Where are you?"

Jupiter landed on Amelia's shoulder and licked her face.

"I know, I know. Let's go find Laural."

Jupiter launched into the air and headed towards the far wall.

Greg clasped Amelia's hand. Her stomach twitched. "You're not going anywhere without me, Mel. All that time I was in the cage...all I could think about was you." Greg turned to face her. "Look, I'm sorry for what happened before. If you want to stay here....um...I'll miss you but I get it... using a wheelchair...um...I understand."

Amelia's heart pounded so hard she thought it was going to burst. "I'm not mad. I'm...ahhh...sorry too. We'd better go. Jupiter's left without us."

Her face was crimson, she just knew it. *I blew it. I should have told him I'd miss him too.* "I see Jupiter. Follow me." Amelia ran hand in hand with Greg, dodging celebrating nus.

Finally, they escaped the crowd. Jupiter led them to the north tip of Gatineve. He hovered a couple inches from the sand, spinning his rotors. Sand spewed in every direction, and Amelia caught a brief glimpse of silver on the ground. She swiped the rest of the sand away, revealing a wooden trapdoor with a gleaming handle.

Amelia pulled it open. Sweet-smelling brown smoke surrounded them and formed a ladder leading down into the hole.

Jupiter disappeared down the hole. "Hey, wait for us!" Amelia shouted.

"It looks pretty dark down there, Mel, are you sure it's safe?"

Amelia folded her arms. "Sheesh, did you forget lesson number one already? Trust!"

She started to climb down and heard Greg's voice above her. "I can't believe you're the same person who didn't want to go camping, Mel."

"That's because I'm not!"

CHAPTER 33

They reached the bottom of the ladder and stood side by side.
"It's just like my dream!" Amelia said softly.

Twinkling lights filled a dark underground cave. Up ahead, Amelia could see a bright light shining like a spotlight on a hill. There in the middle of the hill stood a majestic banyan tree, its green leaves larger than Amelia and Greg. Its trunk was made up of twisted roots, and its branches stretched in all directions.

"C'mon." Amelia started up the hill. The ground below her feet changed from green to white as they went higher. Jupiter waited for them, fluttering next to a crevice in the tree, which was emanating a flickering fire.

When they reached the Sneed, Amelia realized with a start that it wasn't a flame at all. It was Laural's red hair!

Amelia held up her hand, aiming her wrist at the crevice. "Please work!" A flash of green sprang out of the Ayer, hit the crevice, and Laural appeared. She was slightly bigger than Jupiter with iridescent wings.

"She's a fairy!" Greg crowed.

"I am most certainly *not* a fairy," Laural snapped.

"Oh...uh...sorry. So, what are you?"

"I'm a Nelea. Bold, beautiful and, thanks to Amelia, free!"

"I knew you could do it, Amelia." Laural flitted around Amelia's head. "Thank you! Thank you! And look at my face! The mask is gone!" Laural pinched her own cheeks. "Ooo, I missed these pudgy cheeks."

163

Jupiter started to buzz and kiss Laural's cheeks. "Jupiter! Jupiter! I missed you, too."

The Nelea dashed to Amelia and tapped her nose. "I'm so glad you finally remembered me."

Amelia opened her mouth to speak, but Laural placed her tiny hand on Amelia's lips. "Shhh. Let's get out of here!"

Laural and Jupiter led the way to the ladder.

Greg said, "So you're a wizard? That's awesome, Mel. Strange—but really cool."

"Yeah, it's weird, all right."

"Did it take you long to learn how to fly and shoot spells? You really seem good at it."

"I wasn't thrilled about flying at first. I had a little help from an eccentric wizard."

"Still, you're lucky."

"I suppose. I'm lucky because I...ah...have a...Queen Fredonia is my grandmother, Sri is my mother, and Meesha is my brother. They're my family."

"Grandma K. and I have always been your family too, Mel."

"Yeah, of course you have."

"C'mon, let's catch up, Mel." Greg took off running.

Amelia flew ahead of him and stood at the bottom of the ladder with her arms crossed, grinning.

"Hey!" Greg was panting.

"Beat ya!"

When they returned to Gatineve, they found the celebration had grown. Tables loaded with food sat outside every tent. Pieces of the masks had been gathered and thrown into a huge bonfire.

Winston and Grandma K. sat with Meesha enjoying tall glasses of lime juice. Meesha ran to Amelia. "Look what Sri...er...I mean Mom gave me!" He held up an Ayer. It had fourteen beads all gleaming in the light. "It's a wizard's Ayer!"

"You're a wizard!" Amelia hugged him. "You're what you wished to be."

"Yep! I'm like you, sister." Meesha stepped back and bowed to Amelia. "I can't wait until you teach me how to do all those spells."

"Just remember the blue one is for healing. I have a feeling you're going to need that one a lot while you're learning how to fly." Amelia tousled Meesha's hair.

Before Meesha could protest, they heard a low, rumbling noise like thunder, followed by flashes of neon green and yellow across the sky.

"Look!" Greg pointed to a red String, swirling, twisting and turning like a live wire.

The wind blew stronger with each twist of the glowing String.

Grandma K. grabbed for her cap. "What is it, Greg?"

"Grandma K., I think it's time for us to go home."

"In that thing? It's..." Grandma K. was talking to Amelia, but the girl was listening to Winston.

Now what? Are you staying with us?

Greg grabbed Amelia's hand. "It was unfair of me to expect you to go back to your life using the wheelchair, Mel. I can't possibly understand what it was like. And... well... you have a family here." Greg's eyes met hers. "It's just...uh...I'll really miss you."

Amelia smiled. She leaned in and kissed him on the cheek. "I'll miss you to Earth and back, Greg."

He hugged her. "Don't worry, I'll look out for Joey. I'll tell him stories about our adventure."

Joey. She had made him a promise. But the wheelchair....

Greg cleared his throat. "Thank you for saving me, Mel. Jerry Rice and Joe Montana all over again, right?"

Amelia nodded. Grandma K. put her arm around her. "Boy, did I miss good ol' E-town, but y'know, sweetie, I learned, home is here." Grandma K. pointed to her heart. "We'll see each other agin—I just know it. You take care." Grandma took Greg's hand. "Gregory, we need to let this dear girl go to her destiny."

Sri, Winston, and Meesha were standing beside her. Amelia knew this was the moment. She had to choose.

"Only you know your path, Amelia," said Winston.

Leave her mother and brother—the real family she'd been yearning for since she was a child? Return to life using a wheelchair now that she could fly? It made no sense. "Can't they stay here with us?" she asked. "Make Greg and Grandma K. stay."

Sri stroked her daughter's hair. "What's important is right now, not what *might* happen later. The answer is inside you, and you already know it. So follow the whisper, Amelia."

"Queen Fredonia and my sister could be on Earth."

"Yes, Amelia, and so could Ralient."

"How will I find them if I go?"

"The hows are not important. Following your path is what is important, daughter."

"I'm supposed to go. I know it now. I want to go."

"You will be missed, but remember I'm only a thought away." Sri hugged Amelia.

"Amelia!" Meesha grabbed her. "But, why?"

"It's hard to explain, Meesha, other than I just know this is the right decision. Please try and understand."

Meesha frowned but hugged her. "I wish you'd stay."

"I'm sorry. Trust that we will see each other again. Who knows, maybe I'll find our sister and bring her back."

Meesha nodded. "Always together."

"You have grown more than I expected." Winston's voice showered over her from behind. Amelia gazed at Winston.

"Thank you."

The light caught Winston's eyes, and she saw tears glistening on his amber fur. Amelia bowed to Sri and Winston.

"The String is ready. Go! Hurry before it disappears!" Sri waved her on.

Amelia ran faster than she had ever run in her life. She ran because she could, and she was thankful for every step, knowing they would soon be her last. But she didn't care. Sitting or standing, she was the same Mel.

"Greg, I've been thinking, you'll never pass algebra without my help. Besides who's going to insult you and keep your head from bursting off your shoulders when you score all those touchdowns?"

Greg faced her. Those blue eyes! She kept talking. "Did you know our school has adaptive track? You'll never keep up when I get my racing wheelchair."

Greg scooped her up into his arms and spun her around. Her cheeks burned as bright as the light within her.

Winston yelled, "Think of me when you have your first piece of shoo fly pie!"

"You betcha, big one. How could I ever forget *you*?"

Greg set her down.

Grandma K. threw her Phillies hat into the air and shouted, "E-town, here we come!"

All three waved good-bye to the cheering crowd. Red light danced around them. Amelia would miss Mystic, but she knew this wasn't good-bye forever. *I'm exactly where I'm supposed to be.*

Together they raised their arms, shouted, "Whooooeeee!" and jumped into the light.

Made in the USA
Columbia, SC
15 January 2018